Yellowstone
Sabotage

C. R. Fulton

D0886008

THE CAMPGROUND KIDS
www.bakkenbooks.com

ISBN 978-1-955657-42-6
For Worldwide Distribution
Printed in the U.S.A.

Published by Bakken Books
2023
www.bakkenbooks.com

*To every park ranger and first responder
who has taken risks to help someone in need,
you make the world a better place!*

National Park Adventures: Series One
Grand Teton Stampede
Smoky Mountain Survival
Zion Gold Rush
Rocky Mountain Challenge
Grand Canyon Rescue

National Park Adventures: Series Two
Yellowstone Sabotage
Yosemite Fortune
Acadia Discovery
Glacier Vanishing
Arches Legend

For more books, check out:
www.bakkenbooks.com

- 1 -

"Dad, why are you swerving?" my little sister Sadie asks, her brown eyes worried.

Leaning forward, I see Dad gripping the wheel so hard it might break.

"I'm not, Honey. I think we just blew a tire."

"Oh, no!" Mom looks down at the map in her lap. Two full days of driving have gotten us to the middle of Nowhere, USA.

A loud *thwap, thwap, thwap* makes Ethan shout, *"What is happening?"*

As Dad wrestles the lurching truck to the side of the highway, I grip the seat ahead of me to keep my head from hitting the window. We bump to a stop, and I need a minute to breathe normally again.

"Okay, it could be worse," comments Ethan, who is built like a string bean. He shifts in the middle seat next to me. "We could have caused a ten-car pileup and taken out the guardrail!"

"Thanks for the doom-and-gloom report," I say dryly.

"Anytime...anytime." He runs a hand through his shaggy hair.

"Isaiah," Dad says, his eyes on mine in the rearview mirror. "Let's get the spare put on."

I nod, but my body is frozen, and my heart is pounding. The truck rocks from the wind of a semi zooming by.

"Greg, can't we get off the road a little farther?" Mom asks, her face pale.

By the time Dad has eased the truck into the grass, I've convinced my legs to move, breaking the statue-like grip of fear over my body.

"Wait for it..." Dad says, watching the traffic zipping past. "Now!"

He gets out of the truck, and I do the same, managing not to fall because of my rubbery muscles. We head to the passenger side around the truck bed full of our camping gear, and I groan when I see the damage.

The tire is shredded with steel and rubber cords exposed at odd angles. The steel belts of the ruined tire had damaged the wheel well and cracked the fender. I saw places where the glossy black paint had been scratched.

"Oh, Dad, the fender is ruined!"

His wide hand grips my shoulder. "I'm just thankful we are all right. The parts are replaceable; my family is not."

"But... But..." I sputter, my heart sinking as I study the damage.

Ethan hops out. "Where is the spare?"

Dad crouches, peering beneath the truck bed. "Under here."

I look out over the dry, scrubby plains of Nebraska that seem to go on forever. I shiver in the warm sun, thinking of how far we are from anywhere. Dad pops the hood and unhooks the jack.

"Can I get the spare down?" I ask, longing to do something important like he does.

"You can try. It might be tough to break loose."

"Yes!" I grab the wrench he hands me and crawl underneath the truck bed. Gravel pokes my back as I fit the tool to the metal nut holding up the spare tire. I push as hard as I can, but it won't budge. Grimacing, I lock my knee against the truck frame and groan as I try again. "Come on!"

My muscles are now screaming but trying hard gains me nothing.

"Got it?" Dad asks as he cranks the jack.

"No," I sigh. *Why can't I ever do big things? I'm tired of being just a kid. I wish I was older.*

"Here, let me crack it loose." He eases under the truck next to me, takes the wrench, and strains until the nut gives way. "There, son! Now you can finish the job."

My arms are still burning, but I force them to turn the wrench, frowning as the tire lowers. The frustration I've felt for months about my shortcomings won't quit eating at me. *I feel worthless.*

"Hand me the tire iron, Ethan." Dad's voice reaches me.

"You mean the quarter-inch crooked *toe bend-*

er?" he squeaks, hopping on one foot after dropping the tool on the other.

The spare tire slowly lowers, then falls the last few inches on my thick chest. *Good thing I'm not any bigger boned or I might be stuck under here.* Another semi speeds past, and the blast of air blows grit into my eyes.

By the time we've got the spare on, Sadie has stuck her head out the door at least five times to ask, "Are you done yet?" *I guess that's what ten-year-olds do.*

"Yes, we're done now," Dad responds to her question. "Let's find somewhere to take a break."

-2-

"Eeehhhaa!" Ethan's long legs churn as he plunges toward a cliff of pure sand. He disappears over the edge, his arms flailing as he tries to maintain his balance.

Grinning, I catapult after him. The hot sand shifts under my bare feet as I rush for the steep drop-off. Hollering as I half fall, half run down the shifting bank of sand, I see Sadie rolling down the last part far below me. Her long brown hair is packed with sand.

Ethan trips, flopping face first, but a massive sand avalanche following him won't let him stop, and he somersaults the rest of the way, bending backward in ways that look painful.

Dad stands at the bottom, smiling at us. "You got it, Isaiah!"

He had been the first to try running down the sand dunes. My legs are tired now, and as gravity forces me to move faster, keeping my balance is harder than I had thought it would be. Somehow, I reach the bottom, still upright.

"What a cool place!" Sadie yells, throwing sand in the air.

"Morrill Sand Pits, Nebraska—the perfect final stop before we reach Yellowstone National Park," Dad says. "Come on, Honey!" he shouts to Mom who is watching near the top.

"I think I'll stay here." She crosses her arms.

"Mom…" Sadie pleads, "We've been in the car for two days! You need to stretch your legs!"

She copies exactly what Mom has been saying during the long drive to the oldest national park on earth.

Ethan rolls to a stop beside me, his shirt twisted tight around his thin frame. His face is plastered on one side with sand. "Yeah, Aunt Ruth. It's a blast!" He croaks on the last word, coughing out sand. Then he shakes his body like a dog. "I'm doing it again!"

He rushes for the dune, but the shifting sand slows him down.

"Me, too!" Sadie cries, having a much better time because she's so much lighter.

We finally reach the top, puffing hard. Dad takes Mom's hand. "It's really fun! Come slide with me, Ruth."

Ethan, Sadie, and I whoop with joy as we leap over the edge. This time I miss the first step and fall on my rear. I pick up speed, sliding snakelike down the steep incline, sand flowing over my arms and legs. "Wahoo!"

Behind me I hear Mom shriek, and without looking, I know Dad "helped" her start down.

Ethan repeats his face flop performance, and I regain my feet at the bottom, turning to see Mom clutching Dad's strong arm, screeching and laughing as they slip and slide down the hill together.

Watching her reminds me of our first camping trip to Grand Teton. I grin at the remembrance... stampedes, stolen horses, and Mom's coming down a cliff in much the same way she is descending this sand dune right now.

What awaits us in Yellowstone? This is our first trip into the backcountry. We won't be at the big campgrounds but hiking into the wilds, carrying all our gear in backpacks. Knowing that I have everything I need is a great feeling. Well, at least I *hope* I do. Visiting this park is a dream come true!

"Ugh!" I grunt as a wad of sand hits me square in the back.

Sadie giggles and then takes off.

"I'll get you for that!" I scoop up a handful of sand and chase her till we're exhausted and collapse in laughter.

"Water," Ethan says. "I'd give anything for some water." My tongue is stuck to the roof of my mouth, and I've never felt so dry.

"Me too," Mom says. "Let's load up and get to Yellowstone!"

-3-

Sand spills from my jeans as we line up in front of the Yellowstone National Park welcome sign. My feet are on the ground only 29 miles from where Kota, the black wolf, stalks the forest at the Grand Tetons! I've been longing for this place. I strain to hear the howl of the Yellowstone pack, but Mom squeezes my shoulder. "Smile!"

With a cheesy grin, Ethan throws up his arms. His hand covers my face as the camera clicks.

"Mom, do it again; Ethan blocked it."

"Oh, honey, there's such a long line," Mom says. Right then, a car horn blares, and somebody yells as if to prove her point. I sigh. *Never, ever, can I get a good serious picture!* We shuffle through the crowd back to the truck, leaving trails of sand. The traffic moves at a snail's pace as we head toward the Old Faithful Visitor and Education Center.

"I wanted to see animals at Yellowstone— not people!" Sadie grumbles; her nose is pressed against the window. Driving from the East Entrance to Old Faithful was supposed to take 1 hour and 17 minutes, but the drive takes us 4 hours. Apparently, a bear sighting miles ahead has caused a major traffic jam, so we sit and wait, listening to Ethan sing.

By the time we pull into the parking lot, I'm ready to burst. The only spot Dad can find is the farthest one from the famous geyser. I dive for my gear, but Ethan stretches, moaning in delight, blocking my way. I push past him, only to find my pack is stuck. "Ethan, help me out here."

"In a minute," he says, staring at a man working on a giant antenna in the back of a truck bed.

"I don't have a minute," I force out the words as I struggle to free my pack. I can't risk ripping the strap at the start of what I know will be the most epic adventure of my life.

———

"Okay." He turns, unhooking the strap and then looks back suspiciously toward the truck. "Where did *he* go?"

I heft my pack, excitement tingling. "Who cares, Ethan? Let's go!"

But for Mom and Dad to be ready to leave seems to take an age.

"Come on!" I urge, but the tone of my voice earns me a correction. Finally, I'm set free to explore Yellowstone.

The weather is colder than I had expected, and the mountains still wear a cloak of bright snow on their sides. A cloud overshadows us, and I study the darkening sky. The park stretches for miles in each direction with sites to see including geysers, mudpots, and hot springs, as well as bears, buffalo, and elk. *The place is perfect—rain or shine!*

"The weather report is calling for heavy showers this afternoon, so let's try to get our first camp set up by then." Dad points to the Lone Star Geyser Trail, leading us into the hills.

"But, Dad, Old Faithful is right there!" Sadie points dramatically across the vast parking lot at

———

the wide, steaming plain coated in an odd-looking white crust.

"We just missed an eruption," Dad says. "The next one could be 120 minutes from now, and it's getting late."

I groan, longing to see water shoot 150 feet into the air. "We'll wait…"

When Dad pins me with a sharp look, I say, "Sorry," not really meaning it. *I sure wanted to see Old Faithful first.*

"The first rule of backpacking is safety. We'll have all week to catch Old Faithful in action."

Ethan struggles to get his backpack on. He circles as he reaches and searches for the drooping strap. Then he trips, and the heavy pack pulls him over. He looks like a turtle on its back. He scrambles, arms and legs flailing, but still misses the dangling strap. I finally grab it, holding it high for him, and in the end, he slips his arm through the shoulder strap.

"Thanks, Isaiah," Ethan says.

Itching for adventure, I turn, waiting for the others to start down the trail.

"Umm…best cousin in the entire world, could you help me up?"

Shaking my head, I turn back and haul him to his feet. "I'll remember that 'best-cousin-in-the-entire-world' bit," I say, smiling.

Our feet crunch on the gravelly trail, and soon we come to a stream. "This is Myriad Creek," Dad says as he sits down to pull off his hiking boots. There's no bridge, so I do the same as Dad so we can keep our boots dry. Ethan, however, is already in the knee-deep water, stomping around the creek. The water is icy cold, and I suck in a sharp breath as the current tugs at me.

Ethan is eating a power bar by the time the rest of us have our boots back on. He squishes down the trail ahead, his shoes bubbling with every step.

"Look!" Sadie says excitedly. "We are now witnessing our first mudpot. I shall name it *Ethanera Mudpoticus.*"

Ethan dances around as he declares, "I'm finally famous!"

"You know, I read that Yellowstone has over half the world's geothermal features," Mom says. I notice her hiking sticks are keeping rhythm with her stride.

"That's what we planned; but with that sky being so black, I think we should get right to site OA2." Dad sticks to his decision, and deep down, I know he's right. We've got to respect the environment here. It's not like our neighborhood in Kentucky. "I'm already regretting setting such a long hike for day one after such a late start," Dad adds.

"You can't predict the weather or the traffic jams arranged by bears! Besides, we will have lots of days to see all the geysers in this section of the park," Mom soothes.

"Exactly how far of a hike are we talking about?" Ethan asks suspiciously.

"Three and a half miles," Dad says easily.

"Three? I'm not sure I signed up for this!" Ethan wails.

"You didn't have to," Sadie responds sweetly. "You're family, so you don't have a choice!"

"Aw, thanks. When you put it that way, let's go!"

A dirt trail, hedged in by knee-deep grass, winds into the distance. Ethan is still in the lead, and I bunch up close to him, wishing I was first. If I could set the pace, we might have a shot at setting up camp before nightfall.

"Freeze!" He stops so suddenly I crash into his pack.

"Ethan!" I rub my nose, annoyed. But he doesn't respond as he stares at the path ahead.

"Is it a snake?" Mom's voice cracks as she says the words.

"No," Ethan whispers.

I pull down on his arm, which is still spread wide, and peer around him. Then I gasp, frozen just like he is.

"What?" Sadie cries, pushing up under his other arm.

"Oh, my…" she whispers.

-4-

We stare at a paw print like none I've ever seen. The main pad is long and wide; its claw marks extend far beyond the toe pads.

My hushed tone fills with awe as I say, "It's a grizzly!"

We creep forward as quietly as possible. Mom sucks in a long breath when she sees it. I reach out with a trembling finger to touch the dampened earth, smashed by the creature's massive weight.

"I was not aware they came that large," Dad says. Spreading his hand over the print doesn't begin to cover the animal track.

Mom turns, carefully scanning the rolling hills. "Are we sure we want to do this?"

I swallow hard past the tension in my throat. "Pretty sure…"

"How long ago was that animal here?" she asks.

I blink quickly, as knowledge from my tracking game books surface.

"No…n…not that long ago, Mom," I answer truthfully. "See how there's almost no dampness inside the print? However, because the soil all around is very wet from all the rain here lately, the bear probably left this track within the hour."

I look up to find Ethan clutching his bottle of bear spray repellent.

"Um, Ethan? Are you intending to shoot yourself with that spray?"

"No, of course not! That bear had better not come anywhere near me, or I'll show him a thing or two."

"Like how easy it is to catch boys who've rendered themselves useless by shooting bear spray up their nose?" I point to the nozzle. Hastily, he turns the bottle, a flush of red creeping up his neck.

"Let's take some pictures with this print," Dad interrupts. "Seeing this huge print might turn out to be one of the most amazing experiences we have seen while camping."

When we're done posing, Ethan has loosened up a little, so he eases himself into a push-up position above the print. He sucks in another long breath. "It's as wide as my chest!"

He's got a point there! In fact, the print might be wider than he is. "That means you should work out more."

"Honey…" Mom chides.

I shrug as Dad shifts his heavy pack. "Let's hope this bear isn't heading to site OA2."

We set off with a bit more caution in our step and with Dad positioned in the lead. We've covered about a mile, and my legs are feeling the strain of the large pack. But the print makes me push forward, scanning the lodgepole pine trees for sections of brown fur.

"*Sha!*" Ethan's arms spread wide again, the color draining from his face. My hair stands on end as I follow his rigid gaze.

-5-

Not 50 yards away is the massive outline of brown fur I've been expecting to see. I stop breathing as the fur shifts, and the sun glints off something...horns. *It's a bear with horns!*

"Bu...buffalo..." Mom stammers, her shoulders sagging as she places one hand over her heart. I suck in a long overdue breath as the massive bull shakes his head. A cloud of flies rises and then lands on his nose again.

"Actually, that's a common misconception. We are looking at a *bison*—not a buffalo. A few key differences between the two include the large shoulder hump, the beard, and the shaggy hair on their shoulders and head, which a buffalo lacks," Sadie says with one finger held up in the air, proud of her knowledge from her animal studies.

"Well, I'm just happy it's not spelled B-E-A-R!" Mom swats at a mosquito that must be the size of a quarter.

I slap at the cloud of bugs gathering around me and watch as the muscular creature fades into the trees.

"That's the closest I've ever seen a bison!" Sadie squeals. "He was so fluffy!" Her hands are at her mouth, elbows tight against her sides in delight.

"Actually, most of him looked quite bald," Ethan quips.

Mom laughs. "You're right, Ethan. The hair on his back half looked like it had a buzz cut, but he surely was hairy on his shoulders."

Ethan effects a radio announcer voice. "And the animal kingdom winner for the funkiest hairdo goes to the American bison."

I smack my neck, frowning as I look at my palm and see both a mosquito and a black fly. *I'll give Yellowstone one thing; it's got plenty of creatures that like to bite!*

"Here, let's put on this spray. It's completely safe for the environment." Mom pulls out her essential oil bug spray, and I forget to hold my breath while she sprays my head. I cough hard, tasting plants.

"Mmm…minty fresh," Ethan sniffs. "Now even the elk will want to eat us."

Mom rolls her eyes as she sprays everyone. "Let's keep moving. The rain is getting closer. I can smell it along with the peppermint."

I test the air. I catch a faint whiff of the fresh smell that comes before rain. "You're right!"

All of us groan at the black clouds, knowing the coming storm could make for a long, chilly night. With every step we take, my pack feels heavier. Ethan and Sadie are experiencing the same because Sadie is huffing, and Ethan is asking, "How much farther, Uncle Greg? I'm not sure I can make it another mile."

"Five more minutes," Dad says.

"That's what you said in the truck on the way here—except it was two days."

"Five minutes sounds better, doesn't it?"

-6-

By the time we reach site OA2, I'm exhausted. The sky is spitting on me, but we have truly arrived in the wild. The campsite is only a small clearing with no signs of civilization.

I notice Sadie standing by a lodgepole pine, "Hello there!" she says.

I look over at Ethan, shaking my head. "Now she's talking to *trees*," I murmur quietly.

"I am not! I'm talking to *her*."

Ethan and I walk over to see. No one is definitely around. "Sadie, are you feeling okay?"

She rolls her eyes, pointing. "See? Right there?"

I flinch, catching sight of an enormous spider. "Whoa!"

"I don't see anything," Ethan declares. "Are you

two…uhhh…" He finally spots the spider. *Ehhh-hhh!* His long legs scramble, tangling as he skitters backward away from the spider.

"Don't you like spiders, Ethan?" Sadie asks sweetly.

He doesn't answer until he's halfway across the clearing. "Never have, never will!"

"Don't do that!" I say as Sadie reaches for the brilliant yellow-and-black creature.

"She's *only* a yellow garden spider. They can bite, but it has never been recorded that they have bitten a human." The spider's long front legs test Sadie's hand, and then it climbs right on. "See, Isaiah? She's friendly."

I take a few steps back as goosebumps race across my skin. "Maybe she's a he…"

"No," Sadie assures me, holding out her arm so *she* can crawl toward her elbow. "Female spiders are larger, plus they eat the male after mating."

I backpedal a few more steps. Mom suddenly shouts, "Sadie! Put that spider down!"

"All right! Why is everybody so worked up about a little Orb spider?" She gently grasps the yellow striped body and sets it back on its wide web. I notice the web has thick white strands shaped like lightning strikes near the center.

"Isaiah, we are NOT setting up our tent over there," Ethan declares, as he stands with his hands on his hips.

"Fine, how about right here?" I ask, pointing to a level spot far from the web.

"Perfect!"

I haul the tent out of my pack, and we work togther to set it up.

"What did the beaver say to the tree?" Ethan asks as we stash our gear inside.

"Do I have to answer?"

"Absolutely!"

"Timber?"

"No," he says, as he zips the tent.

When he adds nothing more, I roll my eyes. "Okay, what did he say, Ethan?"

He grins. "I knew the answer would be irresistible! I'll tell you if you give me that last piece of gum in your pocket."

"How did you...how could you?" I groan. *Ethan always knows if I have food.* "Fine," I grumble.

He happily takes the gum. "It was nice *gnawing* you! *Ha-ha!*"

"Should have kept the gum," I mutter to myself as the sky breaks loose. We run for the tent Dad, Mom, and Sadie share. Mom opens packets of dehydrated meals and adds water.

Ethan falls backward onto Sadie's sleeping bag, groaning. "Ugh, it smells so good! Just give it to me cold!"

Mom laughs as she sets it over a small foldable propane burner right outside the mesh door. "It will only be a minute, and if this rain keeps up, we will all be glad we've had a hot meal."

The sound of squishing footsteps makes me peer past Mom. "Another hiker!"

I watch a tall, slim man set up a small tent. He doesn't hurry, so I guess he's already soaked.

After a warm meal, I snuggle deep inside my

sleeping bag, feeling perfectly at home in my tent. However, Ethan is shifting around like always.

"Are you ever going to stop wiggling?"

"I'm getting comfortable; it's a very important part of camping," he murmurs as his sleeping bag contorts like a fat caterpillar. Five more minutes pass, and I would have been fast asleep to the pit-ter-patter sound of rain on the tent but for Ethan's continued rolling around. I hear his sleeping bag scrape against the tent fabric. Though one of my favorite sounds, it's now getting old.

"Ethan!"

"Okay, okay, I'm…" he wrestles with the bag once more, "…finally comfy." Stillness overtakes the tent, and a smile forms on my face as I drift off to sleep for the first time in Yellowstone National Park. I knew *backcountry camping* would be great, but I didn't expect the tingle of excitement in my spine!

-7-

"Did you feel that?" Ethan's harsh whisper awakens me from a deep sleep.

"You mean how it will feel when I clobber you for waking me up so early?" I joke.

"No. There! The ground is shaking."

I blink slowly. "Nope. Should I clobber you now?"

An indistinct sound makes me grip my sleeping bag. The rumble seems to rise from the damp earth right under the tent. Ethan sits up stiff as a board, his eyes wide. Now a deep pounding vibrates in our ears.

"You know what that sounds like?" he whispers.

"*Zion*...the avalanches," I whisper in awe. My hands are now spread on the tent bottom, where the tremors seem to race straight toward my heart.

At the same time, Ethan and I dive for the tent opening, mostly getting in each other's way as we fumble for the zipper.

Finally, we trip into the dimness of early morning. Heavy fog hugs OA2, and we can barely see the other tents.

Ethan grips my arm, his face pale. We detect an even louder scraping sound and then the sharp crack of a tree breaking in half. The campsite is so peaceful, but clearly the rest of Yellowstone is less than happy. Everything is soaked. The rain must've lasted all night, and my clothes are already damp from the misty air.

Ethan makes a strangled sound, pointing at something moving in the fog.

"Take it easy, Ethan. It's just the man who camped here last night," I say, covering my own jolt of fear as he emerges from the mist. He has thick brown hair with a small patch of gray near his temples. He waves at us, smiling.

"Um, sir, do you think that was an avalanche?" Ethan asks.

The man comes closer. "It was probably a mudslide that started as an earthquake."

Ethan elbows me. "Told you so."

"You felt it? That's impressive! My seismometer measured it as a 0.8 on the Richter scale. Most people don't feel them that small." He lofts a small metal ball with a digital readout.

Ethan pats my arm. "Being *most people* is okay, Isaiah…if they have an *Ethan* around."

"Right."

The man smiles wider. "I'm Dr. Yniguez. "

My eyes widen at the name. *There's no way I can say that correctly!*

Ethan, however, is another story. "Ynnnigises? Nigezez?" He shakes his head. "I'm E t h a n," he says, drawing out his name like it might be hard to pronounce. "This is Isaiah. Say, since you're a doctor, can you look at this blister I developed on the bottom of my foot yesterday?"

"Sorry, I'm not that kind of a doctor, E t h a n. You see, I have a doctorate in both geology and archaeology. So, really, I'm quite underqualified to look at your blister. But it sure is nice to meet you boys. Do you spend much time in the backcountry?"

"This is our sixth time to go camping at a national park," I answer, "but this is our first time actually backpacking."

"I'd love to hear about your adventures," the doctor says.

"Aw, I ought to write a book about our adventures." Ethan smacks his arm, "Missed!" he says, as a large mosquito buzzes past.

A zipper zings in the still air, and Sadie emerges followed by Mom and Dad.

I gesture toward our visitor. "This is Dr....?" I feel red flushing my cheeks, but he simply smiles and shakes Dad's hand.

"I'm Hans Yniguez. Most folks call me Dr. Y."

"Nice to meet you." Dad introduces my family, and we all fall silent when another deep popping sound rends the air.

"Now that was a rockslide. Over the last three days, nearly five inches of rain has fallen in Yellowstone. That much rain can wreak havoc in the wilderness," Dr. Y says, looking over his shoulder.

Mom nods. "The weather is calling for a beautiful day today, though."

"Yes." Dr. Y stares suspiciously at the mountains.

"It's the snowpack that concerns me," he utters to himself more than to us.

Sadie doesn't miss his mention of snow. "Snow? I love snow!" Sadie exclaims, her eyes gleaming.

He chuckles at her enthusiasm. "Winter never let's go of Yellowstone without a fight. Even though it's June, we've had a cold, wet spring. At higher elevations, the snow is still quite deep. This rain, though, will force it to melt fast—probably too fast."

Ethan's stomach rumbles so loud we can all hear it.

Dr. Y waves as he heads toward his tent, calling back over his shoulder, "It was very nice to make your acquaintance."

We turn, gathering around the tiny propane stove, watching Mom add water to oatmeal. Ethan eats two power bars before breakfast is ready.

"We should have brought a pack mule just for Ethan's food," Dad comments.

"Yes!" Sadie yells, "Could we?"

"NO!" declares Mom.

After we eat, Mom points at Dr. Y's tent. "Oh, my, he looks sore—like he's had an accident."

It's true; as he works at taking down his small one-man tent, he seems to have trouble bending over to reach the ground.

"Can we go help him, Mom?" Sadie asks.

"Sure, honey. Helping him would be nice."

We jog over to the site. "Here, Dr. Y., we'll pack your tent for you," I offer.

"Yeah, we're professional tent packers," Ethan states confidently.

"Ah," Dr. Y grimaces as he straightens. "Your help would be greatly appreciated. I had back surgery three weeks ago, so I'm still a little stiff."

Sadie gathers the poles and sets them neatly on the tent fabric. Then Ethan and I fold and roll the fabric tight. Sadie holds out the bag, but I take it from her. "Here, I got it."

She rolls her eyes, but it's better if I just do it myself. I zip the bag shut easily and hand it to Dr. Y.

"Wow, you are good at that! It hasn't fit that neatly for years. Thank you." He tucks the tent into his hiking pack and hefts it onto his shoulders.

"Doesn't carrying that pack also hurt your back?" Sadie asks.

"No, it's just when I bend down. Besides this pack

is a good friend of mine. We've spent a lot of camping seasons together. Thanks for your help, but I'm off to continue my research."

I wave as he strides down the path. *Research...now that's something important—something big and exactly the opposite of anything I can do.* With a heavy sigh, I turn back to camp.

"Oh, ow! Ohhh..." Ethan is gobbling a cinnamon roll from a roasting stick. "Yum!"

"I warned you the roll was hot," Mom says as she hands me one.

"It's...ow! It's so worth it!" Ethan says around another steaming bite. I blow on mine, but Sadie frowns at hers. I notice the white frosting that's on ours is missing from hers.

"Mooommmm..." she groans.

Mom hugs her. "We can't risk turning you into Sugar Sadie way out here, Honey. Look, I don't have any frosting on mine either, see? Besides, I didn't bring many treats like this; they're too hard to fit in my pack, so let's enjoy them while we have them."

I can't hold back a laugh. "Remember when you cartwheeled across that roof at survival camp?"

A shaky smile turns Sadie's frown.

"Then you turned into a monkey?" Ethan adds.

"I did not," she insists with a grin.

"Oh, yeah, *you did*."

"All right." Dad licks his fingers clean. "Let's break camp. Today we're going to see Old Faithful!"

"Yes!" Sadie, Ethan, and I shout in unison.

We pack up the tents, which makes me long for actual work like Dr. Y's. I wish I'd asked him more about what he does.

Ethan is circling again, chasing the second strap on his pack.

"Here, let me prevent another turtle experience," I say, holding up the strap for him.

"I could've gotten up," he insists.

"Prove it!"

"Fine, *easy*." Ethan lowers himself to a sitting position and then falls back into his pack. "See?" he says as he strains against the chest straps. "I can…" He twists sideways, but the pack doesn't budge. Now his legs and arms are flailing too.

"Ethan, are you all right?" Mom asks as she tucks the tiny propane stove into her pack.

―――――

"Yeah, Mom, he's fine; he's just proving my point."

"Okay, I'm stuck," he says flatly.

I shake my head and pull him to his feet.

"Does Old Faithful make a sound when it erupts?" Sadie asks.

Dad frowns at her question. "I'm not sure; let's go find out."

We set off down the trail, going back the way we'd come. But we don't get very far before the snapping of branches in the trees makes us freeze. We have only one creature in mind, and Mom's face goes white as the sound comes nearer.

―――――

-8-

A loud groan makes me flinch. Ethan takes off back toward camp screaming, *"Eeehhh!"*

I blink and catch sight of a bright-blue strip of fabric.

"It's Dr. Y!" I say in relief as he frees his pack from a low-hanging branch.

"Greg, you'd better go find Ethan," Mom says, and Dad jogs back toward camp.

"Dr. Y, what did you discover?" Mom asks.

He steps out onto the trail. "Something most unexpected…Firehole River has flooded."

Dad returns with Ethan as I consider Dr. Y's message. I say, "But we had to cross Firehole River to get here."

"Excellent point! That leaves us all rather in…a pickle of sorts because the bridge over the creek has washed out," explained Dr. Y.

Sadie gasps, and my eyes go wide, remembering how sturdy the bridge had felt as we had crossed.

"I'd like to see it for myself," Dad says.

"Mind if I accompany you?" Dr. Y asks.

"Not at all."

"Excuse me, Dr. Y., but what type of research are you conducting?" *I hope my vocabulary will impress him.*

"It's a study of ground deformation and its effects on the elevations of large bodies of water and other hydrothermal features."

Well, he just blew my vocabulary out of the water—without trying.

"Can we get that in English, please?" Ethan asks.

Dr. Y smiles. "Yes, of course. I'm measuring the height of the ground."

"Why? It's not like the ground changes," Ethan says, clearly bummed.

"In Yellowstone, it does. Last year we tracked a five-inch rise in the area surrounding Yellowstone

Lake, which shifted the body of water to the east, killing a young forest there."

"But how could it move like that?" I ask, hungry for answers.

"Simple. We are standing on a supervolcano."

My mouth falls open. "Excuse me?"

Dr. Y shrugs. "Yes, Yellowstone is one of the largest supervolcanoes on the planet."

"WHAT!?" Ethan shouts.

"Take it easy." Mom pats Ethan's shoulder.

"Take it easy? When we're in extreme danger? What were we thinking coming here?"

"With nearly 5 million visitors last year, I think we're safe," Sadie adds.

Dr. Y's brows lift. "Nice fact, young lady. You're right. Yellowstone is currently a dormant volcano."

"Hang on a minute!" Ethan snaps his fingers. "Soooo, all these geysers and mudpots are because of the volcano?"

"You got it. In fact, most of the rock in Yellowstone is lava rock."

"No way!" He breathes excitedly, throwing his arms wide open. "I'm…I'm like a superhero! I've slept on a supervolcano! You can now call me *Magma-Man!*"

I shake my head, but before I can say anything, we get our first view of the flooding.

The water is now dark brown in color, and a full-grown tree is sweeping down the river faster than I can run.

"That tree's going to hit the bridge!" I shout right before it slams into the already mangled structure.

I hear a splintering sound, then a deep groan. The thick broken trunk swings toward the far bank, and the current slams it against the dirt embankment. Water gurgles as the massive tree blocks the flow, lodged right where the bridge used to be. We watch as the surging water creeps up the path toward us.

"Come on, kids! Back up a little," Mom says.

"But it didn't rain that much," Sadie says, staring at the destruction.

"Like I said, we had some heavy rains, and now the snowpack is melting. That melting snow also means something else; we probably haven't seen the water levels reach their highest level yet."

"You mean they're going to get even higher?" Ethan squeaks.

The radio beeps. "Dr. Y here."

"This is the park service. Yellowstone National Park is officially closed. I repeat, the park is now closed to visitors due to massive flooding. Evacuate immediately. Alert all visitors that the park is closed, and the greatest caution should be used on any roadway. *Do not access flooded roadways.*"

Our group is wide-eyed, trying to process the squawking radio message.

"B...bu...but we didn't even get to see Old Faithful yet," Ethan sputters as Dr. Y clicks the button to answer.

"Message received." He clears his throat, then continues to speak. "I'm not sure we can—evacuate, that is. Firehole River took out the bridge last night. We're on the campsite spur trail of the Continental Divide."

The radio is silent for a few moments.

"How many people in total?" The fuzzy radio voice asks.

"Six here, but more may be at campsite OA3."

"Dr. Y, do me a favor and get a head count on the entire Firehole Springs area, will you?"

"Roger that." As soon as he clicks off the radio, we explode with questions.

"Do we have to leave?"

"How can we?"

"We just got here!"

"What if we can't get out?"

Then Ethan shouts, "I'm hungry!"

We all stare at him.

"We just ate," Mom says.

"Aw!" He clenches his stomach.

"Folks, I believe we've entered a survival situation. Staying together would be best—at least until I can get a total for the National Park Service."

"Wait, wait, wait!" Sadie says, her hands spread wide, a wild grin appearing on her face. "Do you really mean we're trapped in Yellowstone—as in we have no way out?" Every word comes out all the louder until she's trembling with excitement. "This is the best day ever!" She runs in little circles.

I scowl at Mom. "Are you sure her cinnamon roll didn't have sugar in it?"

"Positive. That's pure Sadie," Mom assures me.

"Sticking together does sound like the best idea. How far is it to OA3?" Dad asks.

Dr. Y shrugs his slim shoulders. "Maybe a quarter of a mile, but the river curves around past that site as well, so I don't believe we'll be able to take the trail to the west either."

"So, we really are trapped here," Dad says.

My stomach feels like it hits my toes as I think through what being trapped means.

"Well, on official trails, yes. But I've got a line of seismometers from here to Shoshone Lake. Possibly we could get out that way."

"Oh, my," Mom whispers, grabbing Sadie as she flashes past.

"Come on, let's see who's camping at OA3."

We chatter the entire way back to our site, but we all fall silent when Dad holds up a fist. In the perfect silence with the mist evaporating, a sound of deep breathing reaches me.

"What is that?" Ethan whispers.

-9-

Dr. Y points to a stand of trees. "Bison. It's the entire herd." His voice nearly dies off before I can catch his reply.

A massive bull emerges from the trees, shaking his head. As he stares us down, he's way too close for comfort. I'd never thought of bison as being quite this intimidating. His head is wider than Dad's shoulders, and his glossy black horns look like they are as sharp as pins. One horn point is crooked, and his muscles ripple as he shakes his head at us.

Dr. Y takes a slow step backward; his hand on my shoulder urging me to do the same. I reach for Sadie, and soon our entire group is creeping backward farther from the bull now pawing the ground. When we get some trees between us, I breathe easier again.

"I call him Abner. He's the boss of Firehole Springs. He's not very good at sharing anything, including space or *air*. Did you know Yellowstone is the only place on earth where bison have always lived? I figure they ought to rule the roost because this is their land," Dr. Y says fondly.

We finally turn and follow Dr. Y over a hill to avoid the herd.

"Sorry for breathing your air, Abner," Ethan says over his shoulder.

Dr. Y smiles. "You kids handled that situation really well."

Mom pats my shoulder. "They practically live at campsites! Plus, they completed survival week in the Rockies last year, and I'm quite confident that Sadie alone could feed us all strictly from wild plants if she had to."

Sadie grins wide, but I frown, wishing I had something special—something real that would make a difference in the world. It's an itch that I can't scratch, and I can't rid myself of the feeling that I'm just too young to do anything important.

Before I can tell him how good I am at building camp shelters, Dr. Y says, "Well, it's good to be in your company."

As we arrive at OA3, I see only one tent.

Dr. Y yells out a cheery hello, causing the tent zipper to be opened.

"Good morning!" A young lady in her 20s calls. A man strides from the treeline, setting down a load of wood.

"I'm Dr. Y." He proceeds to tell them the situation, and they take the news in stride.

"We have provisions for four more days. I guess we'll just sit tight and let the park service take care of people who really need help," the couple says.

"Great! Did anyone else camp here last night?"

"Yes," the man says. "This site allows for six people, and it was full. Three people packed up and headed west. The other camper was a man who kept quiet and to himself, but he left before dawn."

As Dr. Y radios in the total number of campers, the group of three returns, stopping near us.

"The river flooded! You can't take the Continental Divide trail that way," one of them announces excitedly.

"Ah, well, the bridge is also out to the east," Dad says. The faces of the group visibly pale, and my stomach repeats its journey to my toes. *Trapped in Yellowstone.*

"What should we do?"

The radio beeps as if on cue. "Dr. Y, do all 12 hikers have provision for at least a few days?"

"Eleven of us do; I haven't seen the twelfth one."

"Keep a sharp eye out for him. We'll send in a helicopter if anyone needs emergency evacuation."

"YES!" Ethan shouts, his voice echoing long and loud down the valley. A bull elk starts its eerie bugling in response.

"Airlifting you out will be the last option as long as you're safe. We're already swamped trying to empty the park."

"Noooo!" Ethan wails.

"Do not enter any fast-moving water. Even if it looks shallow, strong undercurrents can easily sweep you away. The water temperature is very low, and the melting snowpack has made it even colder than usual. I repeat, stay out of the water! Good luck out there." The radio falls silent.

"Well, I guess we should set up camp again," Mom suggests.

This time, I rush to get my tent set up just right, hoping Dr. Y will notice how I chose a spot that will be both dry and cool.

Dad and Dr. Y are chatting, so I start a fire with my trusty ferro rod, enjoying the bright sparks as they fly toward the tinder.

Soon I'm hanging my tin kettle on a light aluminum frame that holds the pot over the growing flames. I get instant coffee going, remembering when I'd tasted Mom's last year. I shudder at the memory of how bitter it was. Dr. Y, Mom and Dad each have a steaming mug.

"Thank you very much, young man. What a treat!" Dr. Y exclaims.

Sadie comes over, wiping her hands, hiding a brief grin.

"What have you been up to?" I ask, narrowing my eyes.

"Oh, just...you know..." Her grin grows as Ethan enters our tent.

"Wait for it..." Sadie says. "Three, two, one..."

"Eeeeeehhhhhhh!" The tent contorts as Ethan slams into the fabric. "It's on me! It's...*Eeehhhhhh!*" He falls out the door, scrambles up, and takes off running.

Sadie bursts out laughing, bent over, clutching her stomach.

"Did you put that spider in there?" I ask.

"Ye...yesss!" she says around her laughter.

I shake my head, glad it wasn't me who found it.

"I'll go put her back." Sadie wipes her eyes as she eases into our tent. Ethan is in the clearing, repeatedly brushing off his arms and legs.

Sadie has the spider on her head when she comes out.

"She's not afraid of much, is she?" Dr. Y says.

Mom sighs. "No."

"Will you continue your research, Dr. Y?" Dad asks, cradling his mug.

"Yes, I feel I must. This water event could give me data that we've never seen before. I would love to know if the flooding causes any more deformation in the ground. I believe I'll set out to collect my seismometers near Shoshone Lake today. I'm worried the heavy rains might have gotten through the waterproofing. You know, I could use some help gathering my work research equipment. Lately, I've had a bit of trouble that has set me back a few days."

I stare at Dad, desperately hoping he'll say yes to Dr. Y and that we'll get to tag along.

Dad looks at me. "Judging by the look on Isaiah's face, Dr. Y, I had better say yes. So, Isaiah, what do you think about the three of you helping Dr. Y? You would have to do all the heavy lifting and follow his directions exactly."

"M…me? Us? Yes! I mean, I'll go ask them, but it's yes for me!" I might have run over to Ethan; then again, I might have flown. "Ethan, we're helping Dr. Y!"

"We already packed up his tent; what else does he need?" he asks as he eats a huge bite of trail mix.

"Research! We're taking his special trails and seeing Yellowstone like nobody else. Are you in?"

"Twice," he says.

"Wahoo!"

I run to Sadie, but she'd overheard.

"I'll definitely need my bug spray, my medical kit, and extra water." I leave her packing her bag.

"When do we leave?" I say as I skid to a stop near Dr. Y.

"As soon as we're all ready. The water isn't getting any lower, and I'd like to reach my equipment near the shore before it goes under."

"Give me two minutes!" I'm in my tent in a flash, checking to see that my trusty backpack is filled with my usual items: camp shovel, ferro rod, rope, Poppa's knife, an extra set of clothes, food, water, and map. I also check my pockets. I already have a small magnesium fire starter, my trusty dental floss, a bolt, my multi-tool, a small strip of wire, and a pebble.

I hurry Ethan toward Dr. Y and find Sadie already there asking him questions.

"I saw elk, brown bear, bison, fox, and an eagle when I placed this equipment the other day. Hopefully, we'll see even more now."

Mom kisses my forehead and turns to Sadie. "You three be smart and come back safe."

"We will!" we chorus in unison. Setting off with Dr. Y sends a shiver of delight down to my toes. He leads us through the trees where the bison herd had been earlier.

"So, are you a park scientist?" I ask.

"No, but the university I work for sends scientists regularly. Actually, I'm on a personal mission," he says, then falls silent.

"Are you going to leave us in suspense about your mission? I must know!" Ethan cries.

"Oh, yes, no, sorry. I was thinking. A few months ago, I heard about a competition of sorts called the Year of Discovery. A private research firm is looking for a lead scientist to fill a position that would include travel to archaeological sites all over the world, disaster areas, and even ocean study. That position is the kind I've always dreamed of having, but the application process is…well…different. To be considered, I must submit three new discoveries of my own made within the last 12 months."

"Wow!" I breathe, imagining Dr. Y in Egypt uncovering how the pyramids were constructed or in the Amazon at a long-forgotten temple.

"I heard about this position of employment while I was recovering from surgery. But mine wasn't a normal surgery. I had developed a new imaging system, which I then used on myself. The image revealed a pinched nerve and paved an entirely new way for doctors to diagnose nerve problems. When I later read about the contest, I realized I already had completed one discovery. I took some time off from teaching college, and now here we are, changing the world."

"Exactly how are we changing the world?" Ethan asks as he trips on a root and stumbles.

"Good question..." he responds as we crest the top of a hill and gaze out at Yellowstone stretching before us. Sadie gasps then starts counting animals. A combination of elk and a few mule deer are grazing below us in the valley.

"Wow!" Ethan whispers.

Seeing these creatures surviving in the wild is indescribable. I need a full backpack to survive for only a few days, while these incredible animals

———

tough out some of the coldest winters on earth with nothing but their instincts.

"Enjoy the view! The rest of the way we'll be hiking through the woods."

We trek a good distance before Ethan takes up his questioning. "So, this changing-the-world business… How are we going to do that?"

"Ah, yes, *deformation*. That's how."

*"De Fa…*what?"

"It's when the ground deforms from forces beneath. Here, in Yellowstone, magma could be superheating the groundwater."

"And that's…" Sadie starts to speak, but I also have the answer, so I speak over her.

"That's where geysers come from!"

Sadie shrugs at my interruption, but Dr. Y continues. "Yes! But what made the ground rise so much last year? Is it still rising or sinking? Does that mean the volcano is becoming more active?"

"Please say you didn't mean that," Ethan says, halting.

"Don't worry, Ethan. Yellowstone isn't going to do anything drastic just yet."

———

"If you..." Sadie starts to say, but another thought strikes me, and once again, I interrupt.

"Hey, I bet you could really help cities that are affected by volcanoes—maybe even predict what buildings will be most likely to fall."

"Yes, that knowledge could be used in many ways. I just have to get it first!"

"Okay, but the ground doesn't seem squishy," Ethan says, stomping hard with one foot.

"No," Dr. Y laughs, "but if I can discover exactly what causes these movements, my research could be extremely useful for scientists to use in the future. My legwork could help them better predict the occurrence of eruptions on active volcanoes. Then I'll only have one discovery left to make to qualify for that position."

We continue hiking through the trees for a while until I can no longer handle Ethan's looking over his shoulder.

"Ethan, what are you looking for?"

"I feel like somebody is staring at us."

"I don't think you can actually *feel* that," I say, scanning the woods behind us.

———

"I *felt* the earthquake, remember? Don't underestimate my super senses."

"Okay, but it must be an animal. After all, Ethan, there aren't any other people out here."

-10-

Dr. Y. frowns as he surveys Shoshone Lake. I don't see why; the lake is incredibly beautiful. The water appears as smooth as glass, and the blue sky reflects off its surface. Dr. Y's hiking boots crunch along the edge of the water, and the smooth pebbles shift as he walks.

He digs in his pack, pulling out a bulging notebook. When he flips it open, Sadie exclaims, "Whoa!"

He's plastered the pages with different-colored sticky notes. Two flutter into the grass. I pick them up and see one has what looks like a bunch of gibberish written on it. The other contains a diagram of a rock called *feldspar*. "Here you go, Dr. Y."

Dr. Y takes the notes, sticking them back in place, muttering. "No, this is the spot."

He turns a bright-blue note upside down and then right side up. But he's right; the map on it leads straight here—near twin pine trees with two red X's for the seismometers.

Ethan is searching on his hands and knees and suddenly exclaims, "Here's where one was!"

We gather around the small impression in the mud near the grass. It looks like a softball had sat there. "Yes, I set my last one right here."

"Just as I thought—a boot print!" Ethan has a short piece of rope that he uses to carefully measure the print.

"The print could be Dr. Y's from when he placed it here," Sadie comments.

She might be right; the print is faded and has no detail at all.

"We can tell easy enough." Ethan holds out his hand. "Boot, please."

Dr. Y stands, pointing his mud-covered shoe at Ethan. He stretches the rope, but it only reaches from the toe to halfway down Dr. Y's heel.

"No way did *he* leave that print," Ethan declares.

I rub my chest as a familiar feeling races across it. *Something's wrong. That warning in my chest is never wrong.* "Someone took the seismometers."

"Why? Who would want it?" Sadie chews her bottom lip, scowling at the print.

"I...I *really* needed that data." Dr. Y rubs his face with a deep sigh.

Ethan, Sadie, and I look at each other. Without a word, we nod. This is a mystery we've got to help solve. We scatter, and Sadie heads to the right, carefully searching for more prints.

I peek at Dr. Y's notes, then walk toward the other "X." He'd set this one closer to the water and possibly the lake had swallowed it as the water level rose from the flood.

I pull off my boots. As I step into the cold water, I suck in a sharp breath. I wade back and forth until my feet are numb. I cannot find any evidence of a seismometer.

Scanning the shore, I don't see Ethan. I am about to shout at him when he appears at the edge of the woods, eating a granola bar.

"Where were you?" Sadie asks Ethan. As I stumble toward my shoes, my feet like blocks of ice.

"Just checking on a theory," he says cryptically.

Dr. Y pulls a thermometer from his pack and dips the tip in the lake. "Hmm, six degrees colder than average for this time of year."

"Why is that?" Sadie asks as Dr. Y notes the number on a sticky note.

"The snowpacks are melting. The flood waters are running extra cold. I wonder if the temperatures will affect the breeding season of the brown trout." He jots down the question on yet another sticky note. "I sure would love to get a temperature reading on Yellowstone Lake. It has over 650 thermal vents in it. Well, I guess Shoshone Lake was a flop. I suppose we could see if Minute Man Geyser will give us a show."

"YES!" we shout excitedly, bringing a smile to Dr. Y's face.

We pick up the trail, and soon I can see a white cone shape rising near the lake's edge. All around it, a white crust of minerals marks the area. A lazy swirl of steam rises from the cone.

"Ah! Perfect timing! It's about to blow," Dr. Y explains.

"How on earth can you tell?" Ethan's nose wrinkles as he studies the clear pool surrounding the geyser.

Dr. Y. points into the distance. "See that water jumping there?"

"I didn't know planet Earth was the original squirt gun!" Ethan says as we watch hot water shoot from a hole near the trees.

"Never thought of it in that way," Dr. Y. says, "When that *indicator spring* is active, the main geyser is priming."

Sure enough, a burbling sound rumbles deep within Minute Man's cone, then gallons of steaming water shoot skyward. Sometimes the gushes go straight up and sometimes sideways.

A stiff wind off the lake makes me shiver. I turn, scanning the path behind us.

"Is that...?" I squint. The wind is forcing the steam to circle behind us as I blurt out, "I thought I saw a man back there!"

Dr. Y quickly glances in that direction, but by

then the figure is gone. He pulls a small kit from his pack. "Let's test this geyser's heat and acidity."

Sadie gets to pinch a small glass vial in tongs and lower it into the pool. She holds it while Ethan quickly takes its temperature.

"210°! That's hot!"

"Isaiah, put this litmus paper in the sample for two seconds and then match it on this chart."

I accept a thin strip of paper from Dr. Y. As soon as I set it in the sample, it turns bright red. "Whoa! How did it change color?"

"The paper is soaked in a litmus solution, and when the treated paper touches liquid, the litmus reacts to either acid or alkaline."

"*Elk line?*" Ethan asks, his brows knit.

"No, *alkaline*—the opposite of acid. Either one can burn you, so be sure not to touch water from hot springs or geysers."

I match the color to the small chart. "Dr. Y, this spring is as acid as it gets."

"Yes, if an animal dies in a hot spring, its body will dissolve in a day or so without a trace. The acid is very strong."

Ethan rubs his chin, "I wonder what would happen to a seismometer if you tossed it in there?"

"It would take longer, but the acid would eventually dissolve it as well."

"Plus, it would be illegal to do in a national park." Sadie puts her hands on her hips.

We all lean forward and look deep into the steaming pool. That feeling hits me in the chest again, and I look over my shoulder as Dr. Y packs up the samples.

-11-

Right before we reach OA2, we find another grizzly print. This one is not nearly as large as the first one, but it's close to camp—*really close.*

I hug Mom as Dr. Y gathers all 11 campers near our tent. "Let's go over some basic bear safety rules. Don't cook at your tents and don't throw out dirty dishwater near your site. All the food must be kept in a bag suspended from a load-bearing branch high in the trees. That branch needs to be ten feet from the ground and eight feet from the tree trunk. If you have anything edible at all stored in your packs, take out that food and put it in the sack you will be hanging from the branch. You might want to divide the food into two bags."

Mom leans over and whispers, "We did *everything* wrong yesterday."

Ethan's face goes white as Dr. Y continues. "For now, we're all we have to depend on, so let's get some more food bags up into the trees and obey the rules." Everyone moves to help.

"Trapped in Yellowstone! I can't believe our luck!" Sadie declares happily.

"Hey, who is that?" Ethan juts his chin toward a man starting to set up a tent at the very edge of the clearing.

Dr. Y looks up. "Oh, our twelfth camper has finally arrived." He heads over, and we follow.

A stern expression greets Dr. Y's cheery hello. Dr. Y tells the man about the park service's instructions, but the stranger doesn't offer his name.

"Sir, the rangers need your full name, as we're under a state of emergency.

The man frowns but finally snarls, "Brian Hu."

When he abruptly states his last name, I can't help nodding. After all, he has thick black hair and a certain tightness around his eyes. *He must be at least partially Chinese.*

Ethan elbows me, whispering, "Ha-ha, I knew I was right."

"About what?" I whisper back.

"I said *who* is that?" He snorts at his would-be joke, slapping his leg.

I look up to find Brian's dark eyes fixed on us. "To make light of a given name is a grave insult in my culture," he snarls.

His words make my skin crawl. *He's serious.* I swallow hard, and Sadie steps closer to me.

"I'm sorry, sir. I didn't mean to offend you," Ethan apologizes.

"Ah, you accomplished so much without even trying."

Brian's sharp tone makes me frown. *Ethan hasn't done anything that wrong!*

I glance at my cousin and see his eyes are narrowed with an expression I've never seen before.

"Let me make it up to you by pointing out that you're putting that pole in the wrong clip." Ethan is correct; Hu is snapping the tent pole to the wrong corner clip.

"Okay, let's take it easy here. We've all got to

work together," Dr. Y says, pulling us back to our tents. But Ethan turns, nodding when Hu straightens out the fabric and has to unclip the pole.

"Told you…" Ethan whispers under his breath.

Dr. Y radios in the info about the arrival of our missing camper and then turns to us. "Let's go check the river levels; it's not too far."

My legs are longing for a break, but Mom is also eager to go, so I stomp down the path too. Ethan stares at Hu as we pass him.

"Ethan, quit that!" I nudge him.

"They're my eyes, and I can look at him if I want to," he retorts.

"The water has risen so much!" Mom exclaims. The Firehole River has now covered all evidence of the bridge, and the huge tree has twisted even more, lodging itself deeper into the embankment. The river has now changed into a rage of frothing water.

"Oh, no!" Dr. Y's voice trembles as Mom gasps.

-12-

I search the riverbank but see nothing to cause them such distress.

"No! No! Oh, no!" Dr. Y is staring hard upriver, and I catch a fleeting glint of metal in the water.

"Somebody's car!" Sadie shouts.

She's right! A red four-door is sweeping down Firehole River and connects with the roots of the tree wedged in what remains of the bridge. As the car spins wildly in the churning, turbulent water, a pale face stares out the splintered rear window.

"NO!" Dr. Y shouts, struggling out of his heavy pack and racing down the flooded bank.

Dad takes off after him as the car hits the wall of whitewater and submerges. Mom screams, and

I run, my arms pumping, hoping for a glimpse of red paint.

"Hey!" Dad is shouting when the car rockets to the surface. I can hardly breathe when not one, but three faces appear in the rear side window! They're screaming, but I can't hear their voices.

I shove down the fear, drawing up more speed. Far ahead now, the car's fender binds on a mesh of logs; the front of the car whips around as the current crinkles the metal.

Ethan streaks past me, his long legs eating up the distance. I can see Dad and Dr. Y climbing over the mesh of logs entangled in the roots of the tree caught in what's left of the bridge.

As they work their way toward the vehicle, Mom shouts, "Greg, be careful!" Her desperate plea from behind me makes a metallic taste rise in my mouth.

"Dad, wait!" I skid to a halt in the mud, wrenching the rope from my pack.

Dr. Y slips as the logs shift, and water spews up between shifting chunks of wood, leaving just enough room for his body to slip through. The river is running beneath the logs as quickly as it is near the center.

"Hurry!" Dad shouts, diving for Dr. Y's hand as the water sucks him under. Dad's shoulder is submerged before his grim expression changes.

He roars, heaving against the strong current gripping Dr. Y. The logs shift under Dad and only Mom's iron grip on my shoulders prevents me from rushing to help.

"Dad!" Sadie screams.

"Argh!" Dad twists hard, and Dr. Y's head breaks the surface as he gains a desperate breath and then pulls himself from the grip of the river. They scramble back to shore; Dr. Y leans with his hands on his knees, gasping for breath.

"The…car…hurry," he pants, but Dad's already trying another route.

"Greg, the rope!" Mom urges me to throw one end, but she won't let me go any farther.

"Tie it off to a tree!" Dad yells as he catches it and then eases over a tangle of branches as he teeters down the tree trunk where the car is wedged.

I scowl at the car. Only one window shows above

water. I see the three terrified people in the small pocket of air. The fender screeches as the metal is constantly jolted in the current.

Dr. Y follows Dad's steps exactly.

"Why don't they open the window?" Sadie asks.

"The current is too strong. It's just too strong," Ethan mutters, wringing his hands as he paces the bank.

Dad finally reaches the car. Now I can see an old man shouting inside, but the window fogs with his breath. He appears to be holding up two women inside the battered car. The river rages at the car, and everyone screams as the tree rocks hard.

"I need a rock—something to break the window…anything!" Dad yanks on the door handle far underwater so hard he wrenches off the handle, but the door is pinched too hard against the tree to open.

"Something sharp! Hurry!" Dad shouts, tossing away the handle.

Mom and Sadie search along the banks.

I dig in my pack for a sharp object. Frustrated, I finally dump the contents and spot my folding camp shovel! I grab it and race for the water, but Dr. Y has scrambled back, reaching for the tool.

"Stay here!" he shouts, and I groan inwardly at his order. *I can't ever do anything!*

Dad grabs the tool from Dr. Y, hauls back, and drives it into the glass. Only splintered, the people inside are still trapped.

Dad plunges down with the shovel again; this time the shovel goes through the glass, and the water runs red.

"Greg!" Mom's face is pale, but Dad doesn't seem to notice the gash on his arm. He pulls off his shirt, placing it carefully over the broken glass.

"She's hurt! Take her first!" the old man shouts. Despite the rising water swirling at his neck, he is holding a white-haired lady who is completely limp in his arms.

Dr. Y strips off his shirt to help pad the jagged glass, and they struggle to pull her safely through the small, ragged opening.

"Careful!"

"Watch her arm!"

Everybody's shouting at once. Moving the small

woman requires Dad and Dr. Y work together to carry her over the shifting surface. They stagger back to the bank with their burden.

"Ethan!" Dad point-blank shouts, rousing him out of his frozen stare. "Run to camp for help!"

"Right," he barely whispers, then takes off through the trees. He's running so fast I bet he could leap clear over Abner's hump.

"Get her away from the water," Dr. Y orders as they head back to the car again.

The tree shifts, and the car bobs like a buoy. Dr. Y and Dad fall back, barely safe from the seething current.

"NO!" I shout as I help ease the lady to the ground. But Dad is up before I can rush to help him.

Dr. Y reaches the second person, who isn't in much better shape than the first. Soon, two cold pale-faced ladies are lying on the bank. Sadie pulls out a survival blanket, and I test the knot tying the rope to a sturdy tree.

"Hurry, Dad!" I encourage, wishing I was out there beside him, *doing something important.*

The old man is tall, and Dad and Dr. Y heave to get him through the window. The metal shrieks as Dad braces one boot on the window frame and pulls, the veins standing out on his neck. The old man cries in pain as he comes through, but their efforts to free him rips the car loose. It shoots away with the current.

Dad does a momentary split, then plunges into the churning water. The rope snaps tight in my hand.

-13-

Someone is screaming. *It might be me.* Dr. Y struggles with the old man's weight as the tree bobs, now free of the car's weight.

Mom is suddenly next to me, her hands gripping the rope. "PULL, Isaiah!" she screams.

Together, we strain hard. "He's still holding on!" Mom cries.

Sweat pours down my back as we slowly back up the steep hill. Finally, Dad's head breaks the surface. Mom goes wild yanking him to the bank. She's on him in a flash, wrapping him in her arms.

"Isaiah!" Sadie cries. "Dr. Y is in trouble!"

Halfway to the shore, the older man is sagging, his strength gone. As he slips toward the river, I rush forward, sliding on the bark. My knee burns where it scrapes on the tree, but I grab the man's arm right before his legs completely give way.

"Thank God!" Dr. Y's face is red from the strain. Finally, we flop onto the bank, and the man we rescued collapses in the dirt.

Footsteps pound. Ethan is running like the wind, and the rest of the campers are spread out in a V-shape behind him. *All he needs is a cape to really be a superhero!* One camper drops to her knees next to the white-haired lady, pressing her fingertips to her neck.

"Erratic pulse," she mutters, lifting the woman's eyelid. I turn toward Dad, and relief floods me. Mom gathers Sadie and me in her arms, and for a while, all I do is breathe, hanging on to them.

Ethan flops to the dirt beside us. "I'm hungry."

"Ha!" Dad's laugh might be the best sound I've ever heard. "Sure wish my truck was here with all our resupplies we'd planned for midtrip."

"I guess we won't get to them for a while," Mom says, finally releasing me.

"We better help these survivors back to camp,"

Dad says. His skin is like ice, and I wonder how long the other people had been in the water.

"Your arm!" I exclaim. I stare at the deep cut revealed as he turns to me.

"Ah, the glass had to break," Dad says, studying the gash. "It didn't hurt until I looked at it."

The lady Ethan brought turns to examine Dad's arm. "That laceration needs stitches," she says. She picks up a small bag, motioning him over. "I'm a nurse, but I don't have anything for the pain. I'm so sorry."

Mom grimaces as Dad holds out his arm. "It's all right." Still, he groans when she starts stitching the edges of the gash together.

"Ethan, you got any good jokes?" I ask. *Dad sure could use a distraction.*

"Of course, I do. I've got more jokes than a hen has eggs. Hey, Uncle Greg, how do you make a tissue dance?"

"Ummm…" Dad grimaces, sweating even in the cold. "You blow it?"

"No, you put a little boogie in it!"

-14-

It's been six hours, and the rescued people are still icy cold. I poke the fire, shifting the wood to give it more air. We had built it as close to my tent as possible, since I had given mine to Rob, Penny, and Hazel. *They surely need it more than I do.* Penny, the oldest lady, still hasn't opened her eyes.

Dr. Y sits across the fire, staring into the light. A frown flickers across his face. The rest of the 12 campers huddle around other fires though some are in my tent helping Penny and Hazel. Hu sits with his back toward us.

Ethan steps into the clearing. His eyes narrow as soon as he sees Hu. He puts two fingers up to his eyes, then rotates them to point at Hu's eyes. *I'm watching you.* Hu scowls back at him. Their mutual hostility makes me uneasy. *I've never seen Ethan dislike someone so much.*

Shrugging, I ask, "Dr. Y, do you have any other equipment in the park?"

"Hmm, what? Oh, yes, I do. I suppose if I want to discover anything new, it's my last hope."

Hu shifts, turning slightly to face us, and Ethan hurries our way.

"Where are they?"

"I set them at Ke…"

"WELL!" Ethan fairly shouts right in the middle of Dr. Y's sentence. "I saw old Abner on my restroom trip. His entire herd is right over the hill. I held my breath, and he seemed to appreciate it."

I scowl at Ethan for interrupting, but he continues. "What did Father Buffalo say to his son when he left for college?"

It's so quiet I can hear a squirrel munching pine nuts on site 0A2.

"Bison," Ethan says, and Dr. Y bursts out laughing at the joke.

"Bye, son," Dr. Y repeats and nods, wiping a

tear from his eye. "Thanks Ethan, I really needed a laugh." He opens his bulging notebook and starts shifting sticky notes into different positions. "Sure wish I had that data."

Mel steps out of the tent. "Is the radio working yet?" Her voice is thick and tense.

It's sitting in pieces on a rock near the fire. It was supposed to be waterproof, but the charging portal was open when Dr. Y tested Firehole River.

He tilts the circuit board in the fading sunset. "Not yet, it's still damp. Things aren't looking very good in there?" He nods toward the tent.

Mel steps farther from the tent, her voice low. "Penny needs immediate medical attention; she's still unconscious. Everything I've done is not enough. Rob is a diabetic, but his insulin was in the car. I've been trying to keep him stable with food, but that won't last too long. If the radio isn't working by morning, someone will have to hike out."

"Um, did you see the river?" I ask, tension coiling in my stomach.

Mel casts a glance down at me, then turns back to Dr. Y. "I'm serious."

He sighs. "Can we wait till morning, or should I start now?"

Mel crosses her arms, swallowing hard. "Nobody should move at night in Yellowstone. Morning will have to do."

"You're right." He nods, staring at the radio.

Mom calls Ethan and me over to the tent, and we squeeze in. She's sitting with one hand resting on Dad's shoulder.

"Thank God we're all together tonight," she says. I lean into Dad's one-armed hug, trying to block out images of the rope pulled tight in the swirling water. Ethan stares at nothing.

"Are you all right?" Mom asks him.

He frowns, tears shimmering in his eyes. "Mostly. I mean, most of the time. I'm good with water—after what happened to me at Grand Teton National Park." He takes a deep breath. "But today, I couldn't get myself to go near the bank—not even when you all desperately needed my help." He looks down at the sleeping bags.

"You ran for help, and that was exactly what we needed," Dad encourages.

"Ethan," Mom says in that soft voice she uses when she is sharing something important. "You have two choices. Two roads are in front of you, but you can only travel on one at a time. You can carry today, plus what happened at the Tetons along with you all the time. You can replay it in your mind and in your dreams. Every time you see rough water, you'll get a shock of fear and wonder if you'll be brave enough next time. These memories will live inside of you and grow, becoming a part of who you are. As those memories grow stronger, you'll be giving them power over your future.

"Or you can decide to think about how you and Uncle Greg both survived and shut down the memory of the fear. And the fear will grow smaller and smaller. You're the only one who can guard your thoughts. Your job is to think good, positive thoughts. You alone can choose what you take with you into the future."

Mom's words sink in deep inside of me.

Ethan presses his fingertips together and says, "Aunt Ruth, before I had a chicken, but now you've taught me to lay eggs."

A second goes by as I roll his statement around in my mind. Then we all burst out laughing.

Mom covers her mouth, smothering her laughter. "Oh, Ethan, I love you. Come here." She hugs him tight, then pulls in Sadie and me. Dad joins the group hug, wrapping all of us in his arms.

"Ethan, I think you meant: if you give a man a fish, he eats for a day. But if you teach a man to fish, he can eat for a lifetime," Dad says.

"Yeah, yeah, you said it better, though."

When we finally settle down, we feel like packaged sardines inside a can. I remind myself I'm happy that my tent is being used by people who need it more than we do. Ethan elbows me as he tries to "get comfortable."

"Hey, not going to lay an egg on me, are you?" I ask.

Sadie falls into another fit of laughter.

"I meant, you know, she taught me how to accomplish something on my own! I'm never going to live that one down, am I?"

"Nope, probably not. But if you start clucking, I'm going to run."

He elbows me again.

We take a long time to fall asleep because Ethan is muttering earthquake measurements. "0.8...0.9...0.6...0.12."

"Ethan," Dad says in the pitch dark, "the last one was bigger! Even I felt it. I think you should've said 1.2."

"Oh, you're right! That's what I meant—1.2."

-15-

I must have managed to fall asleep somehow because my eyes snap open wide. Everything is still as I search for what awakened me. *Boom!*

I grip my sleeping bag, wishing Ethan was still commenting on tremors.

Boom!

The soft pounding only comes every so often. I strain to see in the dark. Then an earthy scent reaches me—one that's wild, *alive.* The memory of bear prints makes sweat drip down my temples.

I feel a heavy rush of air, another blast, and the tent fabric wobbles near my head at the bottom. My eyes are adjusting, and I can barely make out the forms of my sleeping family.

Dad shifts, sitting up on one elbow.

"Shhh…" I barely breathe as our eyes shine in the dim light. Slowly, he reaches with his injured arm to clutch a can of bear spray.

I flinch hard, as fur rubs against the tent an inch from my shoulder. My motion wakes Ethan, who moans, causing an agitated movement outside.

I clamp my hand over his mouth. Something pointy flexes the tent. Then the clouds must have cleared from the moon because we can see Abner's silhouette against the thin fabric.

Boom!

He's pawing right beside my head. Dad holds out a fist, and I know he wants me to be still. But remaining still as the massive animal looms over me takes all the courage I have.

When we'd pulled the tent out of the brush at the Grand Tetons, I had marveled at how easily the creatures had demolished it. But now, with Abner's massive bulk beside me, I don't know what to do.

He rakes his horn harder against the tent, making a zipping sound. I leap back to avoid it and land squarely on Sadie.

"Ow! Hey…" Dad's hand clamps over her mouth, and I hold up a finger to my lips as Abner's shadow jumps. The ground seems to tremble as he hops to one side before pushing on the fabric again. Mom's eyes are wide in the dim light.

The moonlight brightens, and I can see his outline again as he shakes his head vigorously with his tail held straight up in the air. The little tuft of hair on the end waves like a flag.

"On three…" Dad whispers, "…roar as loud as you can and hit the tent."

Mom grimaces, and my mouth falls open as dry as can be. Ethan nods rapidly, swallowing hard.

Dad eases up to one knee as Abner's horns nearly pierce the tent.

What will happen if the fabric gets stuck on his horns? I shudder to think.

"One." Dad's lips move with barely a sound, and he shifts Sadie behind him. Abner snorts at the motion, and we all flinch. My chest feels exposed as I'm closest to the beast.

"Two." Dad's eyes are locked on Abner's shadowy form, and suddenly I'm not sure which one is scarier—the massive bison or Dad poised to protect us.

"THREE!" His shout raises goosebumps and makes my hair stand on end. He leaps over Ethan and me till he's between the creature and us. *Dad's roar must register on the Richter scale.* Forcing my voice to join his takes a heartbeat for me. Clouds rush over the moon, and our voices echo in the pitch dark.

Something sweeps hard against the tent, and the opposite side nearly buckles. The moonlight returns, but no more bison shadow haunts our sleep.

Somehow, I'm standing outside the tent, watching as the entire herd rushes into the trees. Abner darts around, forcing stragglers to hurry.

"Dad, we did it!" I shout, as all the other campers scramble from their tents.

"What's going on?" Dr. Y rushes over.

"Ol' Abner paid us a visit. Sorry for the scare," Dad says as he rests one hand on my shoulder.

Dr. Y wipes his forehead. "I'm glad it ended well. You never know with a temperamental bull like Abner."

I grip Dad in a bear hug as tears squeeze from my eyes. I replay his putting himself in front of us. *Someday, I'm going to be just like him.*

Mel steps from my tent. "Good news! All the commotion woke Penny for a moment. She wasn't conscious long, but it was a good sign. Did you try the radio?"

Dr. Y shakes his head. "If I try while it's wet, it will fry the circuits; then we're really done."

Mel nods as she ducks back into the tent.

I look up at Dad. "How did I get out of the tent? I don't even remember moving."

He pats my shoulder. "That's called *adrenaline*. In stressful times, that hormone can give you super strength and speed for a few seconds. Whew!" He feels his chest. "I sure had some flowing too!"

I turn to find Ethan glaring at the far end of camp with his arms crossed. "Uncle Greg, I am going to use…the restroom."

"Sure, don't go too far and watch out for snakes."

I scowl as Ethan weaves through the dark camp, staying low and ducking behind the other tents. *Sure doesn't look like a bathroom trip to me.* He slips his slim frame behind a tree, disappearing deeper into the midnight woods.

I open my mouth to speak, but Sadie nearly knocks me over.

"That was amazing! He was so close. Ahhh!" She dances around in the moonlight. "I'll never forget that experience!"

"Me neither."

"And remember, our job is to stay away from wildlife in the national park—even if they don't do the same…" Mom says as she ushers us back into the tent.

I settle in, staring up at the fabric, replaying how the ground shook when he pawed.

Mom sits up quickly, "Oatmeal!"

"What?" Sadie and I say together.

"I've got about a cup of oatmeal left."

"Um, Mom…it's the middle of the night, and we've got to preserve our food." I say, mostly to my growling stomach.

"No, *the radio*, I bet it would dry out the radio."

By the time we've lowered the bear ropes and opened the food storage containers, Ethan still hasn't reappeared, and I'm getting nervous about where he is.

I scan the deep dark of the woods where the moonlight doesn't penetrate. While Mom and Dr. Y carefully tuck the radio parts into Mom's oatmeal container, Dad and I hoist the bear bags back into the trees.

"WAAIITTT!"

Goosebumps race across my skin at the wild cry that rips through the woods. All my muscles tense as that crazy adrenaline feeling races through my blood.

Ethan bursts from the woods at top speed. "Wait! I need a snack!"

He skids up to Dad and me.

"Ethan…" Dad says with his hand on his chest. "Don't do that again."

"Sorry, Uncle Greg, but I had to have some trail mix."

-16-

Whump. Whump. Whump. The bison is pounding the earth right next to me. I shift, and the sound only intensifies.

"3.2! It's an earthquake!" Ethan cries, drawing me out of my dream. I'm on my feet, head smashed against the top of the tent, heart pounding, staring at Sadie, who's doing the same. The tent fabric shudders. And I finally get it.

"Helicopter!"

We burst out of the tent, scouring the sky. There!" I point at the speck of black growing larger by the second. I turn to find Dr. Y clipping the radio to his belt.

"The oatmeal worked!" I hug Mom, then rush

out into the open to watch the bright-yellow helicopter land in the tight clearing. The lodgepole pines go wild in the prop wash, bending nearly to the ground.

"Isaiah!" Dad's voice is tight as he shouts over the rotor noise. "Help us."

I rush to grip a section of my sleeping bag, which sags with Penny's limp weight. Her white hair looks like a rabbit's tail peeking out through the top. We struggle toward the group of medics who are leaping from the chopper. Two of them take my place as my fingers slip.

I stare at them in awe. Every motion is fast but calm as they clip her into a stretcher. One straps an oxygen mask onto her face. Looking back, I see Dr. Y sagging under Robert's weight as he tries to walk. I rush back, taking his other arm over my shoulder.

Robert is panting hard, and his skin is still icy cold. The paleness of his face makes me so thankful that the rescue helicopter is here.

"I'm ready!" Ethan's hair flaps wildly as he hefts his pack.

"No, they don't have room for us!" Dr. Y shouts over the deafening noise.

"WHAT?" Ethan's eyes are wide as Mel hops into the helicopter after all three patients are inside.

One medic ducks as he carries a heavy-looking black bag to Dr. Y. I can't make out their words, but a moment later he's back in the bird. Dirt pelts my face as it rises, and the crazed thundering fades.

"Is there food in that bag?" Ethan asks in the silence that settles.

"Yes, it's a resupply, plus a fresh radio." Dr. Y unzips it, and we rush for the jerky on top. I barely chew, stuffing the empty wrappers in my pocket.

"He gave us something else," Dr. Y says as we all look at him. "Knowledge. About four miles south of here we may be able to access the Grand Loop Road. They would like us to move over there today since the river is still rising."

"Is there a trail to follow?" Sadie asks around a mouthful. I guess we'd all been hungrier than we had been willing to let on.

"No, ma'am. We'll have to be extra careful. Yellowstone is full of dangers—like steam vents, acid water, and, of course, floods. But the pilot said we should be able to make it across a swampy section."

"I bet there's a sign in front of that swamp," Ethan says.

"I don't think so," Dr. Y says gently.

"Sure, it says parking for frogs only; all others will be *toad*."

Dr. Y bends forward, laughing. "That's another good one!"

I shake my head, muttering, "At least somebody likes his jokes."

"No helicopter ride…" Ethan sighs, as he stares at the empty sky.

-17-

I look down at my legs coated in thick mud up to my knees. Crossing the swamp had been tough. *No, it had been extremely hard.* Ethan lies down on the side of the deserted Grand Loop Road. Sadie and I join him.

"Kids! Come on, don't lie down near the road," Mom says.

"But Yellowstone is closed—no cars and no people for 3471 miles. We are the only 11 people in the entire park," I say, staring blankly at the sky.

"Good fact, but you still need to move."

I groan as I get up, but my pack makes it nearly impossible. Still, I'm determined not to pull an Ethan. Dad pulls him up as Dr. Y points to a sign.

"Well, are you kids up for a little more data collection?"

"Yes, sir!" Sadie says, but Ethan turns, watching the rest of the group as they settle down for a rest.

"I've got a tilt meter near the Kepler Cascades. And it's not too far out of the way."

"I'm ready," I say, elbowing Ethan. He's glaring hard at Hu. The man glares right back.

"Ethan!" I hiss, "what are you doing?"

"I'm communicating." He frowns at Hu and then turns toward Dr. Y. He takes a deep breath to say something but clamps his mouth shut instead. Sadie and I follow Dr. Y. and Ethan.

"What's gotten into him? I've never seen him dislike someone the way he does Mr. Hu," she whispers.

"I know. What's even stranger is that he was going to say something but didn't."

She nods solemnly. "Something's up. We've got to get to the bottom of it."

We hurry forward to catch Dr. Y in midsentence. "...a waterfall, but a *cascade falls* is broken by distinct rock ledges. This one is *really* pretty."

"Wow!" The swollen Firehole River is roaring down the mountainside, and the booming sound alone is incredible. We breathe in the fresh scent of moving water until my heart has fully absorbed the beauty.

"This way…" I barely hear Dr. Y's voice over the water. *I get the feeling that somehow the Kepler Cascades seems sacred.* As we step off the well-beaten path, the scent of pine curls from the ground as we crunch over dry needles.

"Oh, look!" Dr. Y ducks, pointing. A small gray bird peers down at us with one eye. "That is called a Clark's Nutcracker; without them grizzlies would not exist in Yellowstone."

I squint at the small bird. "I surely must've heard you wrong or misunderstood."

"No, it's true. The piercing beak on this unique bird is designed to pry open pinecones to extract its seeds. In fact, this bird can stash up to 100 at one time in a special pouch beneath its tongue. The Clark's Nutcrackers fly around the forest, burying clusters of four or five seeds in the exposed soil. They can "plant" up to 500 of these seeds every hour!

"Exactly four or five?" Sadie is staring at the bird as it rips apart another cone. "Can they count?"

"Apparently. A single Clark's Nutcracker stores tens of thousands of pine seeds for food during the coming winter. The bird often buries them near tree trunks as landmarks and covers them with small stones so they can remember where their food has been stored!"

"And this bird gives grizzlies life…how?" Ethan skeptically asks.

"Well, pine nuts provide one of the main high caloric options for Yellowstone bears; they can pack on five pounds a day. Without them, they wouldn't be able to survive hibernation. Additionally, these little birds constantly plant new forests for the bears."

"Really? How?"

"They often bury their seeds at the right depth for them to germinate and start growing. That means they plant new pine trees that eventually become forests."

"Hey, look! Here's a little rock." Ethan says as he stoops over a flat small flat rock. He flips it over, revealing a hole with some small black objects—pine nuts.

"One, two," Ethan picks them out, finding four. "Dr. Y, I believe your research has an error."

"No, it doesn't." Dr. Y fishes around in the small hole with one finger. "Five!" he says, holding up the final dirt-covered nut.

"Well, one bird's stash is another man's…lunch!" Ethan opens his mouth, but Sadie grabs his hand before he can eat the seeds.

"Ethan! Those seeds belong to a bird!"

"Possession is nine-tenths of the law!" he argues as they wrestle.

"I have no idea what you just said, but in case you haven't thought about it, that is bird food. Besides, Ethan, they're covered in bird spit!"

"Ummm, that's…a good point. Fine." Ethan replaces them in the hole.

"The rock, Ethan." Sadie says, tapping her toe impatiently.

"Right." He settles the little rock on top of the hole. "There—just like I found it. And I am still hungry."

Sadie rolls her eyes. "Perfect," she says, heading over to a patch of clover-like leaves. She plucks some and studies the stems carefully. "This is lemongrass. Think of it like sweet and sour candy, except without the sweet."

"Interesting!" Ethan takes the handful of greens, and I grin, watching his face. He rips off a huge mouthful like a cow. His lips pull back as his cheeks pucker.

"Whooo! Augh!" A shiver runs down his spine.

Sadie calmly munches some. "Ethan, you are so dramatic."

"Kids, look at that." The quiet awe in Dr. Y's voice draws us closer. He is pointing across the river as it leaps and crashes down a series of falls. A wide boulder-strewn hill is speckled with grizzly bears.

"What are they doing?" Ethan asks, forcing down the lemongrass.

-18-

The grizzlies are busily searching among the barren rocks. I count nearly 20 bears, their shoulder humps tinged with golden hair.

"They are eating moths," Dr. Y explains.

"Moths?" My nose wrinkles.

"Yes, miller moths. These moths, commonly known as the adults of the army cutworm, gather on boulders to warm up, but each bear can eat up to 40,000 of these moths per day!"

Ethan's mouth works like it's full of sand. "Forty-thousand moths would be…really chalky."

"Listen, I'm going to climb up for the tilt meter; I'll be right back." Dr. Y tucks his ever-present bulging notebook under his arm as he climbs.

One bear lifts his giant head, his lower lip flapping. His square snout turns in our direction.

"Oh. Um…bears are…uh…excellent swimmers, right?" Ethan goes a shade whiter as he watches a bear scramble to the top of a boulder, his muscles rippling. He lifts his nose high, searching the air. His beady eyes lock on us.

I shove my hands into my pockets, and a shot of fear runs up my spine. *The beef jerky wrappers are still there; even I can smell them now.*

That feeling shrieks across my chest, and I study the river raging between us.

"I think it would sweep him away." I say, more in hope than confidence, as I shove the wrappers deeper into my pocket and pinch the top shut.

The bear studies the river as we back into the thin covering of trees. I see two more bears lift their noses high, searching the air currents above the water. My mouth is so dry I can't speak.

"It's okay. These bears have an excellent food source, and it's not like we have any food scent on us," Sadie says, happily watching the bears.

My lip twitches at her words. I now realize

how foolish I was for not putting my garbage into Mom's sealed bag.

I hiss in my breath as the first bear puts one paw into the river. The pounding water froths white as it curves over his long claws.

"Um, Sadie, maybe you should inform the bear of that," Ethan says as he backs away.

Another warning feeling in my chest makes me clench my fists. The problem is that feeling is never wrong. The bear moans, then licks up a fluttering moth. The easy snack draws him back to foraging among the boulders.

Sadie and Ethan release long sighs of relief. I can't calm down. *Something is wrong.*

I turn, scanning the slopes behind us. With a jolt, I realize a bear could easily be on this side of the roiling river.

"Sadie, what do you call a bear with no ears?"

"I do not know, Ethan, but I bet I'm about to find out," Sadie says dryly.

"You call them *Bs!* Get it? No ears?"

"Ugh," Sadie moans.

A flash of motion makes me flinch. *What?* I

scowl as a pink sticky note drifts to the ground beside me. Now the yellow one flips and spins. Green, blue…they start to rain down all around.

"Guys…" I say.

Sadie and Ethan spin.

"Catch them!" Ethan shouts, leaping for one. He misses, even as more notes are taken by the wind, whipping in the breeze.

"There's no way we can get them all!" Sadie cries, snatching at two.

Ethan is leaping high, his long arms failing to catch even one. I rush forward, gathering them from the ground, reading one. "Eat dinner?"

"The % of H2O is equal to 10," Sadie reads with a confused stare.

Deep inside, another sensation rushes over me. "Wait!" I cry. "Dr. Y would never let this happen; this is all his research!"

We stare at each other as the notes continue to rain down around us. All at once we bolt for the path Dr. Y had taken. "Go!" I shout, as Ethan sprints ahead of me. *I should be first! We must hurry!* We reach a high rocky ledge, and Sadie screams.

-19-

Dr. Y is lying crumpled in a heap, dangerously near its edge.

"Pull him back!" I shout as we skid to his side.

"Careful! He's hurt!" Sadie shouts. A tear slides down her cheek.

When we pull him away from the drop-off, I gasp. He has a cut near his hairline.

Ethan turns, scanning the tight outcropping. Sadie is already pulling out her first-aid kit. "Keep him as straight as possible! We don't know if the fall hurt his back."

I nod, cradling his head while Sadie cleans the wound with an alcohol wipe. I press my trembling fingers against his neck. "His pulse feels fine."

Dr. Y moans, his eyes flutter. "Cindy?"

"Um, no. I'm Isaiah." *This injury might be worse than I thought.*

"Oh." He touches his head. "What happened?"

"I'll tell you what happened," Ethan says, holding up a rock. "Someone knocked you out."

"Ethan!" Sadie says as she squeezes triple antibiotic ointment over the wound. "Only eleven people are in Yellowstone and four of us are here!"

"Five!" he insists, scanning the area and making my skin crawl.

"The rock must have fallen from the cliffs above. Dr. Y, do you think you hurt your back when you fell?" Sadie asks.

He releases a long breath. "My head seems to be the only problem."

Groaning, he strains to sit up as Sadie and I help steady him.

"I'm not sure you should be moving," she says.

"No, I'm all right; I'm thinking more clearly now." He twists gently. "My back is fine...or at least as fine as it was before."

Ethan scoops up Dr. Y's notebook. I notice it's

significantly thinner as two more notes flutter to the ground.

"Did you find your tilt meter?" I ask.

He turns, scanning the barren rock ledge. "*What*…where is it? I was so relieved to see it after the missing seismometers. I was reaching for it, right there…" He shakes his head.

"Dr. Y, you have an enemy." Ethan squats down solemnly, handing over the notebook.

"Oh, no!" Dr. Y reaches for the now-thin volume, his face white. "Losing equipment is one thing, but this is my mastermind."

Sadie bites her lip. "We'll pick them all up. Getting them back in order will take a while."

We help Dr. Y to his feet, but he's still unsteady, so Sadie and I prop him up. Ethan goes down the steep path first, directing us. By the time we're on flat ground, my arms are trembling from Dr. Y's weight.

"Where did they go?!" Sadie cries. Only a few notes are now scattered here and there.

Scowling, I study the area. The bears are still feeding across the flooded cascade, and the air is

filled with the fresh scent of the rushing water.
Where did the notes go?

"Hang on." Ethan bounds up to the ledge; a moment later, he reappears, picking his way down a steep rock fall on the far side of the ledge.

"Just as I thought," he declares. "He stole the tilt meter and then escaped down a second path. While we were helping Dr. Y, he took all the notes that he could find."

"Who did?" Sadie asks.

"Exactly....Hu." Ethan says, resting his hands on his hips.

I pull the wad of notes that I'd collected from my pocket. "I'm sorry we didn't get them all, but we were worried about you."

Dr. Y eases onto a rock. He moans as he opens the book. More than half of the notes are gone.

I step over to the second path. "Ethan, let me see your boot."

He holds up one foot.

"No, I mean the tread."

He stomps over, high-kicking his boot in front of me.

"Ethan," I say, snatching his foot in midair.

"*Eeehhhh!*" He shouts as he loses his balance, but studying the tread of his boot is easier with him lying down.

Sadie comes over. "What are you looking at?"

I jut my chin toward the soft mud where Ethan had come down. "I see two prints. One set is Ethan's."

Her eyes go wide.

"Told you!" Ethan crosses his arms, nodding.

Sadie crouches over the prints, studying them. "Is someone after Dr. Y?"

"The real question is, who?" I add.

"That's what I keep saying." Ethan stands, dusting off. Then he pulls out a string.

"Well, *who* is it then?" Sadie asks.

"Precisely!" Ethan measures the fresh print with his string.

"You make no sense." Sadie shakes her head.

"Well, you said it."

"Said what?" Sadie squeaks, glaring at Ethan.

"No, you didn't say *what*, you said *Hu*."

"Huh? Ethan, tell me what you mean."

"I just did."

"*Why* is someone after Dr. Y?" she demands.

"No, that would be silly. You can't be after yourself. *Hu* is after Dr. Y."

Sadie growls in frustration. "Ethan, this is serious! *Who* is it?"

"Yes." Ethan nods solemnly.

"ETHAN!" Sadie grips his shoulders. "*Who?*"

"I don't know why you keep asking me…since you already know."

She rolls her eyes and says, "Because you haven't told me *who* is after Dr. Y."

"Do I need to tell you if you already know?"

Sadie bends low, her fists clenched, about to blow a fuse.

"I'm still stuck on *why*," I state.

"No, it's not *Y*, it's *Hu*."

"*Eehh!*" Sadie throws her hands in the air.

"Oh!" I snap my fingers. "You mean it is *Hu*?"

"Yes. That's exactly what I've been saying."

Sadie's eyeballs are the size of marshmallows.

"What's his name?" I pound my thigh in thought.

"Why are you asking me?" Smoke might start coming from Sadie's ears.

"She still thinks it's *Y*," Ethan says to me, rolling his eyes.

"Sadie, it's Brian—Brian Hu!" I say.

"How do I know what the guy's last name is?" Sadie all but shouts.

"He's not asking you; he's telling you," Ethan says easily.

"He's not telling me anything!" She stomps her foot.

"Listen carefully, Sadie." I hold out my hands to her. "Remember the twelfth hiker? You know, the guy who isn't very nice?"

"Yeah."

"Well, his name is Brian—*Brian Hu*."

Her face screws up as she lunges for me.

"Stop! Stop and listen! Like H O O—Brian Hu. That's his name!" I shout.

"That's his name?" She comes to a halt, centimeters from my face. "Why didn't you tell me?"

"*Ugh!*" Ethan throws his hands into the air. "The point is that this print is exactly the same length as the print we found near the seismometers—which means Dr. Y's missing data was…sabotaged."

"Sabotaged?" I echo.

"You may have noticed that I've been watching Hu closely."

"I figured you didn't like the guy," Sadie says.

"Thanks for that lack of confidence. From the very first, I knew something was off about him. But when I noticed a shadowy figure following Dr. Y and tracked it, I found a boot print. Then at the seismometers, I knew it was Hu."

"Problem was, I couldn't prove it. When Abner came to camp, I nearly had Brian Hu. He must've stashed the seismometers in the woods nearby. I was only seconds behind him, and I saw him putting something into his pack. I also found the round marks in the soil where they'd been hidden."

"Why?" I rubbed my chin, thoughts flying.

"No, Hu!" Sadie giggles. Then her face grows serious too. "Dr. Y doesn't seem to know Hu, so what's their connection? Why is Hu stealing Dr. Y's work?"

"I have a theory about that…" Ethan says.

A branch suddenly snaps nearby.

-20-

All of us jump and the hair on my arms stands on end. *Which would be worse: Hu or a grizzly?* I step in front of Sadie, and she clutches the back of my shirt.

"And now, he knows that we know. But what he doesn't know is that we know that he knows we know," Ethan whispers, glaring toward the woods.

Dr. Y is sitting on the ground with his head in his hands. The destroyed notebook is in his lap.

Sadie stomps her foot. "It's not right that Dr. Y has worked so hard and now look at him. We've got to help somehow."

"Okay, when we get back, I'll tackle Hu, and you two go through his bags," Ethan says.

"Two wrongs don't make a right," I say, frowning at Dr. Y. "Let's help him back to the main road."

Gingerly, Ethan and I hoist him to his feet. *I wish we knew if he was so pale from the attack or from losing half of his work.*

He starts walking in the wrong direction. I take his elbow. "We need to go this way."

"Oh, right. Of course." He smiles sheepishly.

Sadie, Ethan, and I look at each other, eyes wide. We pass the bears quietly, then amble to where a swirling eddy in the river has taken over the trail. Logs and debris float in the circular current.

Ethan steps into the woods to go around the same way we had come in earlier.

"Wait! What's that?" Sadie is pointing at the jumble of floating debris.

"Driftwood," I say, still holding Dr. Y's elbow.

"No, to the right. See the animal! It's brown."

Spotting one brown thing from another in the jumble is impossible. "Nope. It's probably dead if it's in there."

She rolls her eyes. "It twitched!" she shrieks. "I'm going out to get it."

"Whoa…" I grab her arm. "Remember what happened to Dad? Safety first, Sadie."

"Does anyone have binoculars?" Dr. Y asks as he studies the driftwood.

"The walking hardware store here ought to have some," Ethan wisecracks.

I groan at his tease. "You're in luck, Ethan; they're even on sale today." I quip as I shrug off my pack and dig them out. *I'm just glad that Dr. Y seems stronger.*

He adjusts them, releasing a sharp breath. "I'm afraid we *can't* leave it there."

"Why?" Ethan asks.

"Because…" Dr. Y leans forward, rolling the focus wheel on my binoculars. "It's the most endangered species in the entire U.S."

"What?" Sadie shouts.

"The black-footed ferret was listed as extinct; but in 1981, a ranch dog named Shep came home with one he had killed. Because of that kill, wildlife biologists became involved in preserving the animals. Kids, we've got to get this one to safety even if it is dead; they may want it for cloning."

That comment captures my attention. "They clone ferrets?"

"Sure do. The species' genetic base is very small, so they've been using DNA sequencing and cloning to bring back older genes that were frozen in the 80s. Possibly the scientists may be able to use even older genes from hides in museums. As a matter of fact, Elizabeth Ann, a black-footed ferret, was successfully cloned using preserved cells from a long-dead wild one."

"But how do we rescue that ferret? I don't like the look of that shifting wood," I say.

"I can do it," Sadie asserts.

Dr. Y studies the area. A tree is leaning over the bank, its eroded roots nearly free from the rushing water.

"If I shimmy out on that tree, I can reach him." I can tell that Sadie is determined now.

The river suddenly surges.

"Oh, no!" Sadie's hands cover her mouth.

I still don't see the creature. But then, with a sharp pop, the roots give way, and the leaning tree jolts closer to the water.

"No way am I letting you out onto that tree," I say flatly.

Sadie is rushing along the flooded bank. "If the tree falls, it will crush him!"

I scour the area where the tree would fall and finally see the ferret. "He doesn't look alive."

"Hurry!" Sadie is about to leap onto the logjam.

"No!" I shout. "I've got an idea."

I hear another low groan, and another deep pop makes me flinch. The trunk is only inches away from the water now. The tiny ferret's tail twitches, but the movement could have been caused by the shifting logs underneath it.

"Ethan, get me a long branch and two short ones!" I dig for my survival blanket. It's easy to tear the silvery sheet, and I lay the smaller section on the ground. "Sadie, cut me three strips of rope."

She falls to her knees as Ethan drags a branch closer. I tie the two short sticks at angles, like prongs of a fork.

"Floss!" I say. Sadie rummages in my pack and slaps it into my hand. I lash the survival blanket tight between the branches. Then I loft the tool and rush to the bank. "Ethan, guide the back of the branch." He takes the far end, and I slowly inch it toward the creature. Sadie helps me untangle it after a floating log snags our makeshift net.

"Hurry!" she shouts as the tree groans again.

I shake the net against the log the ferret is draped across. The animal doesn't move.

"Push!" I shout as I shove hard. The tool nearly sinks the logjam as it shifts, and the ferret rolls lifelessly onto the survival blanket.

We haul the branch back, hand over hand.

"Careful!" Dr. Y warns. "He's small and cute, but he's one of the fiercest predators on earth. If he comes around, he will protect himself."

I frown at the long, limp body of the brown-and-black creature. "I don't think that's possible."

But Sadie is already carefully transferring the black-footed ferret to her now-empty backpack."

It's okay." She's shaking as she carefully keeps the survival blanket between herself and the small creature.

The tree crashes into the eddy, and we all flinch in the cold spray of the raging water.

"Dr. Y, what do we do?" Sadie zips all but an inch of the pack, carefully putting it on so it hangs on her chest, cradling the bottom carefully.

I kneel to add her belongings to Ethan's pack.

Dr. Y pulls out his radio, and I'm glad to see some color in his cheeks. *Maybe the rescue was just what he needed to take his mind from his missing research.*

-21-

"Dr. Y to Park Service. We have a highly endangered ferret that's badly injured...or dead," he adds.

The radio crackles to life. "Must be a case of misidentification. No ferrets are living in Yellowstone, sir."

"Well, there's one now. Possibly the flood washed him here. What's the protocol?"

"You're sure he's not a mink or a Fisher cat?"

"110 percent positive."

"Give me five minutes," she replies.

I've only managed to pack half of Sadie's belongings into Ethan's pack by the time the radio crackles again.

"*Revive and Restore* is sending an airlift to the Old Faithful area. Can you be there in an hour?"

"Yes, ma'am!" Dr. Y now has a spark of life in his eye as he tucks the radio in his belt and sets off toward the road.

"Hang on a minute!" Ethan says, searching for his pack strap as always. "Are you telling me that flood victims and ferrets get a helicopter ride, but we still have to walk?"

"Pretty much," Dr. Y replies.

"If you got on a helicopter, you'd be done in Yellowstone," Sadie says like he's crazy for even thinking about the possibility.

"Hadn't considered that angle." Ethan is circling, hunting for the strap as usual. I hold it out for him as always.

"Anyway, I wrote a book about helicopters."

Sadie turns to look at him in disbelief, cradling the injured creature in her pack.

"It really took off!" Ethan nearly loses his balance, laughing at his own joke.

She rolls her eyes. "We've got to hurry. This little guy needs help *right now*."

"Do not open your pack—even if he revives. Ferrets are the fiercest little creatures."

"What about the wolverine?" I ask.

"Pound for pound, this incredible creature would put a wolverine to shame. Ferrets are absolutely fearless, and they spend 95 percent of their time underground hunting prairie dogs."

We hustle to keep up with Sadie.

"Mom!" she shouts, rounding the path. "I need that small blanket!"

We have a time explaining all that has happened during our short excursion. Sadie carefully wraps the blanket around the cold bottom of her pack.

"Isaiah, he's like ice." Her eyes shimmer with tears. "Feel the bottom of the pack."

I put my hand underneath her pack. The bulge in the bottom is deadly cold. "Let's move."

As we set off toward Old Faithful, the rest of our group follows. I turn, counting heads.

"Where's Hu?" I ask Ethan, who's jogging up to join us.

"I just asked Uncle Greg, and he said Hu set off by himself right after we left for the Cascades.

He hiked in the other direction. But I ran down to where Uncle Greg said he was, and as soon as he got out of sight, his tracks cut back toward the Cascade Lake Trail. Nobody's seen him since."

I chew my lip. *If he was willing to hurt Dr. Y, what will he do now? Remain hidden?* Ethan continues to scan the forest along the road.

Sadie maintains the punishing pace as we hike the deserted main road.

"Whew, I need a jetpack to keep up with you!" Ethan pants.

The Visitor Center is within sight when the deep thump of a helicopter breaks the silence.

"We're late!" Sadie shrieks, carefully supporting her pack as she rushes forward.

The chopper settles in the parking lot, and a woman leaps out, ducking the prop wash with a small cage held against her chest. She and Sadie seem so similar; their only concern is the small creature inside her pack.

"I'm Kimberly," she shouts over the noise. "Let's see what you've got there." Wearing thick leather gloves, she reaches into Sadie's bag.

The ferret is still limp as she pulls it from the pack. I am amazed by its long and thin body—almost like a snake with fur and legs, and of course, a super-cute face.

"This *is indeed* a black-footed ferret!" Kimberly exclaims, carefully examining the creature. "Finding this ferret is so strange! They live on prairies almost exclusively eating prairie dogs. They don't live near water. I can't imagine how this one got all the way to Yellowstone! The closest colony of black-footed ferrets is in Meeteetse, Wyoming, 150 miles from here!"

The ferret squeaks faintly, making us all gasp.

"AH! I thought he was long gone! There's no time to waste! Great job, kids!" Kimberly carefully places the creature into the small crate.

"Dr. Y, I'll call you later," she shouts as he finally catches up. Kimberly shields the cage as she jogs back to the helicopter.

I turn, scanning the parking lot. A sinking feeling hits me hard.

-22-

"Dad, where's our truck?"

The vehicle with the long antenna seems lonely as it sits in the center of the lot. Only two other cars remain in the enormous area.

"Oh…" Mom says, frowning.

"I think I see it…" Ethan says slowly.

"Where?" Dad asks.

Ethan points far down the valley.

I gasp when I see one wheel pointing skyward. "No!" I whisper.

"Oh, no, all our food!" Ethan shouts, his hands on his head.

"Well, I guess the scratches on the fenders from the flat won't matter much now," Dad says calmly.

"Do you think he'll be all right?" Sadie asks.

"How could it be?" I snort. "It's flipped over."

"No, I mean the black-footed ferret! We can get another truck, but the ferret means so much to me!"

Leave it to Sadie to only think about the animals.

"One thing is for sure; *Revive and Restore* will do everything they can for him," Mom says as she hugs Sadie tight.

Dr. Y has wandered over to the truck with the long antenna. "Oh, no!" he exclaims.

His cry draws us closer.

"What's wrong?" Sadie asks.

"I'd set my equipment to gather all the satellite data from the strain meters and borehole meters around the park, but it's all been shut down!" A deep red flush creeps up his neck. "This entire trip has been a complete waste of time!"

The rest of our group walks over, and that feeling catches in my chest. *Something's off.* I turn a full circle, searching. Sadie grips my arm, pointing at a lone hiker who is catching up quickly.

"Hu!" I whisper.

"Is that a new owl imitation?" Mom asks.

"Mom," I say, but Hu is too close to say anything else.

"Dr. Y," Ethan says, glaring hard at Hu. "Your work has been sabotaged. The seismometers, the tilt meter at the cascade, and now your truck."

"It's been a truly unfortunate turn of events," Dr. Y agrees. That blank look we saw before has returned to his eyes.

"Unfortunate is when you trip with a Coke in your hand, which ruins your football jersey right before the big game, and you careen into your mom, who was carrying the celebration cupcakes."

Everyone stares at Ethan in open-mouthed wonder.

"I'm speaking from experience here," he says as his eyes narrow even more.

Hu now stands at the edge of our group with his arms crossed, boldly returning Ethan's glare.

"Sabotage is when an enemy deliberately destroys things. Brian Hu is that enemy."

I flinch at his accusation. *What is Ethan doing?* Wishing I was a million miles from here, I cross my arms.

Hu takes a menacing step forward. "Prove it, kid."

"I saw you tinkering with Dr. Y's truck the day we arrived here, plus I took measurements of your boot print, which puts you at the scene of each crime."

"Crime?" Hu has confidence to spare, and suddenly, even I begin to doubt our theory about his interference.

Dr. Y snaps his fingers. "Hold on a minute. Brian Hu? I know that name! You're with Columbia University, aren't you? I read an article of yours on the movement of tectonic plates."

"One and the same," he says easily.

"So, you admit it?" Ethan's voice squeaks.

"I admit my name is Brian Hu. As for your pathetic accusations, you have zero proof. Who will take the word of a kid against mine—a well-known university professor?"

All the frustration boils up. *He's right! We are just a bunch of kids.* I clench my fists together, longing to be older and able.

Ethan growls, and Mom places a hand on his

arm. "Hold on a minute here, boys. I don't think this is the time or place to be having an argument."

"What?" the word explodes. "He's just admitted to being one of Dr. Y's competitors. He even knocked him out with a rock!"

Hu shrugs. "Like I said, you've got nothing on me. I'll be moving on now. Tell the park service I'm well-provisioned."

With that retort, he stalks off.

-23-

If Ethan could bore holes in his back with his eyes, he would.

"Dr. Y, we've got to do something!" I shake his arm, my emotions high. "We can't just let him get away with that!"

"The trouble is, he's right. We can't prove anything," Dr. Y says softly, his shoulders hunched.

I can't stand the thought! It's not fair that he's lost all his work and right under my nose too! When it came down to it, our opinion and our facts hadn't mattered.

"But he could have killed you on that ledge," I insist.

"Isaiah, I honestly don't know what happened

at the Cascades. One minute I was reaching for the tiltmeter, and the next…is all a blur."

I slam my fist into my palm. "I can't ever do anything important! Something *real*."

Dr. Y watches me for a moment until I fidget under his gaze. "Actually, Isaiah, you have a number of qualities that are very desirable in a young man. For instance, if a task is hard, you don't give up like most kids would, and may I add, like most *adults* would. And do you know what that characteristic will eventually bring to you?"

"Uh, more hard things?"

Dr. Y laughs. "No, son. Opportunities! I've been quite impressed by you and your sister." He leans in closer, whispering, "I'm still on the fence about your cousin." *The smile he's hiding tells me otherwise.* "Very impressed. Your willingness to help is something I won't forget." He sighs heavily as I store his words deep inside. "We all face tough times, and we've just got to keep going."

But I can tell it's taking all he has, and my anger at Hu boils like a hot spring about to explode.

Dr. Y starts his truck. The adults form a line to

use his charger for their phones. We've all got plenty of family who are wondering if we're safe.

Ethan climbs into the truck bed to examine the antenna. "Here's what he did!" His cry draws us all forward. "See? He cut these wires."

"I can fix that in a jiffy," Dad says, pulling out his pocket tool. I watch as he strips off the outer coating of plastic, then winds the metal wires together. A few minutes later, a bleep sounds inside the truck.

"It's working! I've got data rolling in!" Dr. Y cries happily. He opens his laptop, and his face goes pale. He reads aloud, "A new article by Brian Hu is taking the scientific world by storm. His research proves ground deformation was affected by the historic flooding of Yellowstone." He flops back in his seat.

"No!" Ethan shouts.

"Mom! We could've had him! Why did you let him get away?" I cry.

"Isaiah." The warning tone in Dad's voice makes me frown. "Your mom was right. If Hu was willing to attack Dr. Y, then we were all in danger with him nearby. Plus, without a law officer present, what were we going to do? Tackle him?"

"Yes!" Ethan shouts. "I'll catch him!"

Dad grabs Ethan's pack. "You'll do no such thing. Dr. Y can press charges after we're all safe."

"So, what now?" Mom asks. "We don't have any way to get out of Yellowstone."

"Yes!" Sadie shouts. "This is the best!"

Mom rolls her eyes.

Dr. Y runs a hand over his pale face. "I'll radio in."

The Park Service informs him that after days of full-time use, the rescue helicopter is down for repairs.

"They think it will be operational tomorrow." The flat tone of defeat in his voice makes me grit my teeth.

"Let's go scavenge what we can from the truck," Dad suggests.

-24-

Ethan plunges a straw into some instant mashed potatoes Mom had gotten from our upside-down truck. Right now, the entire world feels that way—wrong side up.

"Look!" Ethan blows hard, and his mashed potatoes bubble and flop around on his plate. "Now I really am my own mudpot!"

A thick wad of potatoes flings up, sticking to his face.

Sadie falls back, laughing.

But I can't join her—not when Dr. Y won't eat a bite. He's been staring into our fire for hours.

Keeping my voice low, I say, "Listen, we've got to do something." I nod at Dr. Y. "Look at him."

Sadie and Ethan grow serious. "But what?"

"I've been thinking about something Dr. Y said. "Remember how he was worried that water had gotten into the seismometers? We need to double-check Hu's research. I bet his findings are wrong!"

"Yeah, if we could do that, maybe Dr. Y could still come up with a new discovery!" Sadie nods, gobbling her dinner.

"The seismometers might have had an automatic satellite backup. If we could check on that, we would be well on our way to proving that Hu stole them and their data," Ethan offers.

I'm surprised when it's Sadie who hops up and settles next to Dr. Y.

"Could you show me the data from your truck?" she asks boldly as Ethan and I kneel next to them.

"Hmm, what? Oh, I suppose so." He opens a slim laptop and pulls up a map with crazy stripes of color laid over Yellowstone.

"This specialized radar scan of the Earth's surface is called an InSAR map. The process takes very meticulous measurements that are collected from orbiting satellites." He touches some keys, and the screen flashes to a similar map. "See? This is the InSAR map from last year. You can tell how the west side of the park rose, and the east side lowered during that time."

I'm glad he can tell; all I see are rainbow squiggles. "Dr. Y, how do you remember all this stuff?"

"I have a very good mind for details," Dr. Y answers.

Ethan crosses his arms. "You probably got that from learning to spell your last name when you were three." Sadie nods in agreement as Ethan goes on. "Dr. Y, shouldn't your seismometers have backed up to something?"

A puzzled expression makes Dr. Y squint up at the stars. "Well, now that you mention it, yes. But they would have needed to be connected to a computer that could read the data."

"So..." I clear my throat. "If you can find the backups, then you will have absolute proof that Hu stole them."

Dr. Y swallows hard. "That's true."

His finger hovers over an icon with the satellite on it. "Here we go."

The soft sound of his finger tapping the mouse pad makes my skin crawl. A white page full of lines of gibberish fills the screen.

Dr. Y's mouth falls open.

"What?" Sadie clutches his arm.

"Right there—WYNP23. That's the serial number of my set of equipment." His finger trembles as he points to it. The file opens, but it looks like it's been written in Latin.

Dr. Y studies the script, mumbling as he takes in the information. He scrolls for a long time while I chew on my lip, my heart hot against Hu.

"Wait, a minute…" Dr. Y leans forward, intent on the screen. "Look at that!"

One line has been repeated twice.

"Below that line is the same code, but backward," Ethan notes.

Dr. Y's fingers fly over the keys. "Ha! An error code says the seismometers were uncalibrated!"

Dr. Y pulls up different screens so fast I can't even think about reading them.

"In fact…" His nose is nearly pressed against the screen as he scans more lines of code. "The InSAR,

GPS, and my seismometers all have the same error code at the same moment in their history."

"What exactly does that mean?" Sadie asks.

"It must've been a glitch in the satellite system, and it took the programs over three hours to recalibrate and start producing accurate readouts."

"So!" Ethan gleefully slaps his knee. "Hu's article is based on false information!"

"Most likely," Dr. Y says quietly.

"Mom always says that you reap what you sow," I say, feeling like a weight has been lifted from my shoulders.

"I still don't get what that means," Sadie adds.

"Well, Hu stole and cheated, trying to get ahead of Dr. Y. He sowed evil deeds, so, eventually, he got the same returns."

"His scientific reputation may never recover after this report comes out. He should have caught that glitch."

"But he was in too much of a rush to beat you," I say. Dr. Y looks at me sharply.

"I wonder…" His fingers fly over the keys, and I see the list of applicants for the Year of Discovery.

"Brian W. Hu!" I nearly shout. His name is three entries below Dr. Y's name on the list.

Dr. Y closes the page, revealing a map of Yellowstone with green dots scattered over it.

"What's the red one for?" Ethan points to a singular red circle.

"That spot marks the location of a research station that stopped recording data last week. The flood has prevented teams from restoring it."

"It's not far from here," Ethan says. "And I think we make a pretty good team."

Dr. Y looks at us and agrees. "Indeed! I can hardly think of a better one."

"Maybe we should fix it," I venture.

"That idea sounds like a plan."

"Yes!" I shout as Old Faithful explodes skyward, glistening in the moonlight. I watch the steam and water reach 150 feet into the night sky. I feel so much power right below my feet that believing Yellowstone National Park has a few more secrets up her sleeve is easy.

-25-

The research station looks like a tornado tore it apart. A solar panel with wiring sticking out has been torn from its brackets and lies in utter chaos. Two strange-looking boxes sit cockeyed next to a flat area where they should be affixed.

Dr. Y's radio beeps, and he listens to the message: "The helicopter is now functional and should pick you up by 7:00 p.m. tonight. With the current wind conditions, Biscuit Basin is a better location for rendezvous."

"Perfect! We're halfway to Biscuit Basin already." Dr. Y confirms the meeting place, then stares at the wreckage. "This damaged equipment might be more than we can fix."

"I say we try." I flip over the solar panel carefully, finding it still intact. "Ethan, help me boost this up in place."

Sadie helps Dr. Y while Ethan and I struggle to lift the glass panel and place it back in its brackets.

"There. Now, to rewire it." I mutter, recalling how Dad had fixed Dr. Y's antenna.

Carefully, I strip some of the brightly colored coating from the wires. First, I connect the black negative wires, winding them tightly together.

"We'd better check the other end before I connect the red wires."

Dr. Y has the metal boxes set back in place, and I'm pleased to find a simple set of pinch connections for their wiring. "That wasn't as bad as I thought…if these still function," Dr. Y says.

"Here goes nothing." I wind the wires together and flip the switch. A small red light flashes on each box.

"You did it!" Sadie hugs me tight.

"Now, we'll simply reboot." Dr. Y holds down two buttons at once on the boxes, and a soft beep makes me grin.

———

"We've got it!" Dr. Y hurries to link his computer via the USB port.

"Ah-ha! They were still recording on battery power until yesterday!"

His screen loads with a map of the earthquakes that happened during the last week.

"Whoa, there must be hundreds."

"Yes, Yellowstone is always busy creating earthquakes," Dr. Y says.

"Look at that pattern of epicenters!"

His finger traces the Yellowstone River's path. "Let's take a look at the InSAR again."

The strange streaks of color are still meaningless to me. It's sort of like looking at clouds and then seeing shapes in them.

"That looks like a set of wolf tracks!" I point to a distinct trail of darker-colored areas.

"Hold up a minute," Dr. Y says. "You're right." He shifts through the pages again, so Sadie, Ethan and I wander toward the creek.

"Ahem. Nature calls. I'll be right back," Ethan says.

Sadie turns to me. "Isaiah, how are we going to

———

get home? It's hard to believe Dad's truck has been ruined."

I shrug. "I guess we'll have to rent one for a while. But it'll make a great story!"

Ethan steps from the woods, but the snapping of twigs behind him continues.

"Uhh…" My voice freezes as I see a huge shadow stop just beyond Ethan.

"What? It looks like you saw a velociraptor," he says.

"B…bi…bison!" I shout as the massive creature strides into the clearing. Slowly, Ethan turns. The bull is easily taller than he is, and his massive head lowers toward Ethan's chest.

"Oh…hello there. We'll be leaving now," Ethan whispers.

The bull shakes his head, horns glistening, beard flapping. His tail goes straight up in the air, the tuft of hair on the end sticking out like a little flag.

-26-

"Uh-oh," I say.

"I guess I'm breathing your air again, Mr. Bison." Ethan crouches, and I know everything is about to explode.

Ethan takes off with jackrabbit speed, but the bull's rippling muscles propel him forward far faster than Ethan.

"NOOOO!"

I can't tell who's shouting, only that a branch is suddenly in my hand as the bull's horn catches Ethan's pants. I hear a tearing sound and then see a sharp motion as he tosses Ethan into the air.

His long arms flail until he lands hard, crumpling to the ground. The bull spins, springing high with all four legs off the ground, heading for Ethan's still form.

"*Aarrrgggg!*" I roar, surging after the bull. I break the branch over his hindquarters. "Get away from him!" I scream.

I blink, and I see he's now facing me—his new target. Pawing dirt high into the air, he lowers his head, and time slows to a crawl. As his massive shoulders bunch, my skin tingles, but I can't seem to move. He takes two long strides in slow motion, when something hits the bison square on the nose. He turns aside from me.

I flinch, and time snaps back to its frantic pace as Sadie launches another rock. This one hits the bison's flank, raising a poof of dust from his hide.

The bull snorts, then crashes into the forest, and I start to tremble.

"Ethan!" Sadie shouts, rushing forward.

"8.0! 8.0! It was the big one!" Ethan blinks his eyes rapidly.

We help him sit up.

"I'm okay! Really, I'm okay. My pants, however, are not."

I glance behind him to see fabric flapping in the breeze.

Sadie giggles. "Only you, Ethan, only you."

We help Ethan to his feet, and I pull Sadie into a hug. "I didn't know you could throw like that."

"Me neither!"

"Maybe you should try out for baseball."

"Nah, that would take too much time away from camping."

"Good point."

"I hope I didn't hurt him," she says.

"Oh, come on, that bull is just fine."

Dr. Y stands there, his computer dangling forgotten in his hand.

"You three are…" He shakes his head as he searches for the appropriate words. "…some incredible kids."

"Thank you! We accept the compliment," Ethan says as he takes a bow, placing his left hand behind his back. "Ow!" he exclaims as he rubs his back.

I step back to look, "You've got a scrape across your back from the bison's horn."

"Trust me, I feel it. I think he just broke the

skin, though. Let's get out of here before 'Abner the Second' returns."

"I'll get your pack," I say, groaning as I lift it. One arm is easy to hook through the strap, but the other seems to have vanished. I start to circle, reaching for it. I trip on the wire and then land hard on the pack.

Ethan cackles. "Now you know my pain! Let's see you get up."

"Easy," I say, finally locating the second strap. But no matter how hard I strain, I can't get to my feet. Sadie takes my hand and hoists me up.

"I sure am glad my sister is so strong," I say, the image of the bison still too fresh in my mind. "I would have been bison burger."

"Isaiah Rawlings! Was that a joke?" Ethan says.

"Miracles happen."

"Speaking of miracles, look at this!" Dr. Y turns his computer toward us. "That unique anomaly you noted allowed me to detect a comparative analysis with a most interesting outcome!"

"Um… You forgot to speak in English," Sadie says flatly.

"Right. Sorry. Isaiah, you were correct. That trail of dark areas proved to be the exact location of every major mudslide that occurred during the flood."

"Wow!" I say, not quite sure why he is excited about mudslides.

"When I compared the InSAR maps, I discovered a clear shift visible for up to 20 minutes before the actual slides occurred."

"And?" Ethan questions.

"That means we can accurately predict mudslides using InSAR, which could save countless lives every year and…this discovery definitely qualifies as my second groundbreaking one this year!"

"Groundbreaking… That's a good one, Dr. Y. Get it? Mudslides do break ground," Ethan grins.

Dr. Y matches his smile. "Yes, and it's all thanks to you three."

-27-

The hike to Biscuit Basin had been easy.

"Wow!" Sadie and I breathe the word together. A long wooden boardwalk stretches before us, winding through intensely colorful pools of steaming water.

"Will we have time to do the boardwalk?" I ask Mom and Dad.

"The chopper should be here in a little under two hours. Let's go!" Mom says.

"Whoa!" Ethan points. "A geyser is erupting!" Sure enough, white water shoots into the air far down in the valley.

My mouth hangs open in wonder. *Yellowstone is one of the wildest places on earth!*

Mom shifts her huge pack. "All right, troops, let's set out."

Ethan trips, and I catch him by the elbow. "Good start, Cousin!"

"Oops. I must've grown again last night!"

Our feet echo on the boardwalk, and we approach steaming pools to our right. An area covered in white crust surrounds them.

"Black Diamond Pool…" Mom reads on a sign posted near three brilliant blue and yellow pools.

"Black Opal Pool and Wall Pool…" Dad finishes.

"Wall Pool?" Ethan's nose wrinkles. "What kind of name is that?"

The breeze shifts, and the Yellowstone steam engulfs me. The warm mist touches my face, and I feel as if the park has reached out and claimed me for its own. My breath comes faster, and I close my eyes as I breathe it in.

"Oh! It stinks like rotten eggs!" Ethan doubles over, coughing.

"You're ruining the moment," I mutter. He ignores me and staggers forward, waving a hand in front of his face.

"Dad, what makes that smell?" Sadie asks.

"Well, it's actually sulfur present in the ground, and the more acidic the water is, the stronger the odor gets," he explains.

"I don't think it's that bad," Sadie says.

We start forward again, but for me, something's different. I've truly passed into Yellowstone, and a part of me will belong to this place forever. I know I will carry a bit of it with me wherever I go.

"Come on, Isaiah!" Sadie shouts, rushing through the shifting mist. "Look at this yellow stream."

"You mean *Yellowstone*," Ethan states.

"No, I mean *stream*. That's a *yellow* stream!" She points at a small flow of clear water on a streak of brilliant yellow rock, and the sun seems to turn the water into a million little diamonds.

"Okay, so maybe it is *Yellowstone*," she admits.

"Wow, this place is incredible!" Mom exclaims, snapping a picture of the water.

"Sapphire Pool." I read the sign next to a large pool that's neon blue.

"Oh, I read about this one," Mom says. "The water is 200°!"

"How hot is boiling water?" I ask, searching my mind for the answer.

"212°—so the water in this pool is nearly boiling. Plus, this is where the valley got its name. At one time, the accumulation of mineral deposits shaped like biscuits developed all around Sapphire Pool. However, an earthquake and geyser eruption in 1959 blasted away nearly all of the geyserite embellishments," Mom adds.

"Blasted *biscuits?* Nooooo!" Ethan cries.

"Yes." Mom nods solemnly. "Blasted biscuits."

We study the white film of minerals that we've seen near every single hot spring. All the deposits have upwelled from deep within the earth.

"I see one! A non-blasted biscuit!" Ethan leans over the rail. "Oh, it looks so yummy—soft and tender, melt-in-your-mouth buttery biscuits!"

"Uh-oh," Mom says. "Ethan, we're not back to civilization yet, so you're going to have to handle being hungry a little longer."

"No worries, Aunt Ruth." He shrugs out of his pack, unzips the top, shifts through the contents, and pulls out a small bag containing a smashed peanut-butter-and-jelly sandwich that looks as if it had been run over by Abner.

"Eww." Sadie pulls up one side of her lip as Ethan squeezes the contents directly into his mouth.

"Not quite a biscuit, but it will do!"

"There it goes!" Sadie shouts, pointing ahead to a plume of water shooting high into the air.

We rush down the boardwalk watching in awe as Jewel Geyser erupts. Hot water sprays nearly six feet into the air in random gushes. *Yellowstone truly is like no other.*

-28-

Having never been in a helicopter before, I'm surprised by its power as we lift off from Biscuit Basin.

"Wow!" I can't really hear Mom past the ear-muffs we're all wearing, but I can read her lips.

The pilot tilts us forward, and I press my nose to the window, watching Yellowstone sweep past. The river comes into view, and I can't believe how much of the road has been demolished by the flood.

Dr. Y was forced to leave his truck behind. The rangers said there wouldn't be a passable way for him to drive out of the park until the water subsided. Still, he seems quite happy to be viewing the first mudslide from his map.

He's filling out sticky notes as fast as possible. *At this rate, he'll have that notebook bulging again in no time.* When we land at the North Entrance of the park, I'm filled with amazement at the sheer size of Yellowstone. We hustle off the chopper.

"Did you see all the hot springs? Their colors are so amazing!" Sadie cries.

"Isaiah, help me with our gear!" Dad shouts over the sound of the rotors. I rush forward to help him. As soon as we have our belongings in a pile, the chopper takes off. I flop onto our bags, breathless from the effort.

"Dad, why did Hu cheat? What made deception seem acceptable to him?"

As he sits down next to me, the pile shifts. "I've been thinking about that. At the root of everything Hu did was one motive: selfishness. He did it all to promote himself and to get what he wanted. Selfishness never hurts that one person alone; being selfish hurts everyone around them too. Selfishness and pride are two sides of the same coin."

"Pride? You think Hu was proud?"

"Of course. What's right in the middle of the

word *pride?* The letter I. Pride is a stick with two ends. Hubris isn't only thinking you're the best; a prideful person can also think the worst of himself or herself. In short, pride is thinking about *yourself,* and that's exactly what Hu did. He wanted something, and he left no stone unturned to get what he wanted for himself. Funny though, selfishness always seems to backfire. A wise man once said pride goes before a fall."

"Yeah, now he's got humiliation," I say.

"Yes, he does. Hu didn't get this way suddenly, either. He's probably lived his whole life putting himself first and getting ahead by putting others down. What Hu did is no different from a kid's elbowing his sister out of the way..." He adds the last sentence softly.

My gaze snaps up to Dad's. I frown. *Seeing myself alongside Hu isn't very satisfying.* "I didn't think of it that way."

"You know, Isaiah, humans are always the most miserable when they are looking at themselves. Thinking you're the greatest or the worst is a trap we all must guard against and avoid. Statistics and data prove people are happiest when they're helping others."

As usual, I see no judgment in his eyes—only compassion. "Dad, I'm not going to turn out like Brian Hu, I promise."

He pulls me close, and I've never felt so safe. We turn as a park ranger approaches.

"We tried to have a rental vehicle ready for you, but you will need to wait about an hour," she says.

"Thank you!" Mom replies, setting her bag upright on the sidewalk.

Deep inside, my heart constricts at the thought of only one more hour in Yellowstone!

"Oh! Could we become Junior Rangers before we go?" I ask.

The ranger nods. "I was going to deliver booklets and badges to the Visitor's Center, but I haven't been able to get there, so they are still in my truck. You've clearly taken at least one hike in Yellowstone, and I believe right now would qualify as visiting with the park ranger. Just fill out the booklets, and your membership will be official."

"Yes!" I run for Sadie and Ethan, and we start

working straightaway. I enjoy filling in the answers and, even better, the confidence that can only come from knowing how to survive.

Saying the pledge altogether is the perfect ending to this adventure—one that makes me grin happily. I'm pretty sure Mom even sneaks a picture with me smiling. The ranger holds out the first badge. I start to reach for it and then stop.

"Sadie," I say, "That one's for you."

She looks at me sharply, "Really?"

"Yup."

Her smile makes my heart feel warm and full. I glance over to find Dad watching; he nods at me in approval, and the truth hits me. I'd finally done something big and manly, and putting my sister before myself was the smallest act. Inside, I feel older, more complete. The ranger hands Ethan and me ours, and I plan exactly where it should go on my trusty pack with the claw marks. We head back to the rest of the group.

"What's that?" Dr. Y asks, pointing to the arrowhead-shaped badges with Old Faithful front and center.

"It's my sixth Junior Ranger badge. Pretty snazzy, huh?" Ethan holds it out at an angle so Dr. Y can admire it.

Dr. Y. scribbles on one of his ever-present sticky note pads. Then he pulls of the note and slaps it on Ethan's chest.

Ethan scowls down at it. "What's this?"

"It's *my* badge of approval," Dr. Y replies.

Ethan peels off the note to read, "*Junior Scientist Certified by Dr. Y. Sweet!*" He sticks it to his forehead, grinning. Dr. Y hands Sadie and me each a "badge" as well. Mine is yellow, and the paper seems strangely warm in my hands. I rub my thumb over the words, and the black ink seems to wash away that heavy sense of frustration.

The truth is, we had done important things. I won't be a kid forever, but while I am, I plan to enjoy every minute and learn as much as I can.

"Oh, did you know that this…" Dr. Y watches his phone carefully as he takes three huge steps forward. "…is the border of Wyoming and Montana…and also the edge of Yellowstone National Park?"

"No kidding!" Ethan strides forward, spreading his legs wide, so one foot is in Wyoming and one in Montana.

Mom walks by, loading me up with food from the rangers.

"Hey, Ethan," I call.

"Hold on! To which Ethan are you referring? The Montana Ethan or the Wyoming Ethan?"

"Ugh, well, the Montana one, I guess," I say.

"Excuse me…" He jumps high, twisting, until his other side is toward me. He pats his face, "Montana is my good side, anyway."

"Well, here's a power bar. I know you're hungry."

"Two, please!" he says excitedly. "One for each state!"

-29-

Dear Isaiah, Sadie and Ethan,

I talked to Kimberly today, and she had a surprising report that she asked me to share with you. The ferret we rescued survived! In fact, genetic testing has revealed his DNA is 50 percent different from all 600 or so known living black-footed ferrets. This difference means he will add fresh genetic diversity to the captive breeding program and possibly save his species.

They theorize he may have been from an entirely unknown colony, which raises some exciting possibilities for these ferocious little guys. It just goes to show how much we have yet to learn.

Also, I owe you my eternal gratitude. Our mudslide detection theory using InSAR has proven out!

Thanks to my favorite group of Campground Kids, we now have the opportunity to save thousands of lives every year!

Well, I'm off to find my third discovery.

Yours truly,

Dr. Y